Devil
Of The
Night

Table of Contents

Dedication

To the relentless pursuers of truth, the unwavering champions of light against the encroaching darkness, and to those who find courage in the face of unimaginable horror. This story is dedicated to the tireless souls who fight the unseen battles, who stand vigilant against the shadows that lurk in the corners of our world, and in the deeper, darker recesses of the human heart. It's for the hunters who risk everything to protect the innocent, for the warriors who stand against the tide of evil even when victory seems impossible, and for those who bear witness to the unspeakable and still find the strength to carry on. Their strength, their courage, their unwavering commitment to the fight, even when the odds are stacked against them, is the driving force behind this narrative. Their silent sacrifices, their quiet battles, often fought in the hidden spaces of our reality, deserve recognition and understanding.

This dedication also goes out to the victims, those who have fallen prey to the monsters, both material and ethereal, that stalk the night and hide in plain sight. Their stories, often unspoken, are a chilling testament to the darkness that dwells within our world. While this narrative focuses on the hunters, the hunted are always present—a constant reminder of the stakes and the devastating toll of the fight against the shadows. Their memory serves as a powerful reminder of the urgency of the battle, and the critical importance of standing firm against the overwhelming power of evil. Their silent screams echo in the streets, their unseen pain, a constant presence, their existence, a shadow woven into the fabric of this very tale.

Finally, this is dedicated to the dreamers, the writers, the artists, those who dare to confront their own darkness, to translate the fears that lurk beneath the surface of reality into stories that resonate and that offer a glimpse into the unseen. We, the storytellers, carry the torch of the hunted and the hunters, and in doing so we confront our own shadows. It is through this process, the exploration of our own darkness, that we can truly illuminate the courage and sacrifice of those who fight the battles we can only imagine. This book, born from the darkness, is a testament to the enduring power of hope in the face of despair, and the enduring human spirit in the heart of horror.

Chapter 1: The Crimson Fog

The reek of stale urine and decay clung to the air like a second skin, a fitting aroma for the alleyway where Mike first saw him. Salt Lake City, usually a beacon of Mormon piety and gleaming modernity, revealed its festering underbelly in this forgotten space. The moon, a sliver of bone in the inky sky, cast long, skeletal shadows that danced with the unnatural crimson fog swirling around the corner. It wasn't the typical Salt Lake fog, the damp, grey shroud of a mountain winter. This was something else entirely – thick, viscous, a sentient tide of blood-red mist that pulsed with an almost malevolent breath.

Mike, his face a roadmap of scars earned in countless battles against the undead, gripped his customized .44 Magnum tighter. His breath hitched in his throat, a familiar knot of dread tightening in his chest. Years of hunting vampires had dulled the edge of fear, but this…this was different. The fog itself felt wrong, an intrusion, a living entity pressing against him, its chill seeping into his bones. He'd faced many vampires, but the aura emanating from this crimson cloud was uniquely disturbing.

He'd seen the victims before, scattered through the city's underbelly – the subtle draining, the unnatural pallor, the vacant stare. But he'd never witnessed the act itself, never seen the moment of transformation, the utter violation. This time, he would.

From the swirling fog, a figure emerged – tall, gaunt, impossibly elegant even in its predatory grace. Samson Bordeau. The name sent a shiver down Mike's spine; a name whispered in hushed tones among vampire hunters, a legend built on a trail of terror. He was elegant, almost aristocratic in a macabre fashion, his movements fluid, devoid of the stiff, jerky motions of the lesser vampires. The fog clung to him like a shroud, obscuring his features, yet enhancing the terrifying aura of power and danger he projected.

The victim, a young woman, her eyes wide with a terror that mirrored Mike's own growing dread, lay huddled against the grimy brick wall. She didn't scream, didn't even whimper, as if the fog itself had silenced her, choked the very sound from her lungs. Samson moved with a speed that defied the human eye, a blur of motion against the crimson backdrop. Mike caught glimpses of pale skin, razor-sharp teeth, eyes that gleamed with a cold, predatory light.

It happened so fast, a brutal ballet of death performed in the heart of the swirling fog. One moment, the woman was there, the next, she was empty, drained of life, her body left limp and cold, a husk of its former self. The crimson fog seemed to writhe, to feed off her essence, growing momentarily denser, richer, more intensely red.

Mike, despite his years of experience, felt a wave of nausea wash over him. The sheer brutality, the efficiency, the inhuman grace of it all…it was a sickening spectacle. He knew then that this wasn't just a vampire. This was something far more sinister, something ancient and powerful, something that had tapped into something far darker than mere bloodlust. He felt the cold kiss of the fog on his face, its icy breath a stark reminder of the danger that lurked within its crimson depths.

The fog began to recede, slowly pulling back like a curtain, leaving Samson standing in the eerie silence of the alleyway. His eyes, now clearly visible, fixed on Mike, an unnerving intensity in their cold depths. There was a strange satisfaction in his gaze, a hint of amusement, as if he knew he had been observed, as if he had been waiting for this encounter.

Mike knew he was outmatched. This wasn't some street-level bloodsucker; this was a force of nature, an entity wrapped in crimson fog. But the weariness in his eyes was replaced by a steely resolve. He wasn't afraid of dying, not anymore. He'd seen too much death, endured too much loss, to be consumed by fear. He had a job to do. He had a city to protect. This encounter, though terrifying, only strengthened his resolve.

The crimson fog swirled and shifted, a living, breathing entity that whispered promises of death and destruction. It pulsed with an energy that seemed to resonate with the ancient stones of the city itself, hinting at a power far older than even Samson Bordeau. Mike, for the first time in his long career, felt a sense of genuine, overwhelming dread. This wasn't just a hunt; it was a war. And the war had just begun.

He holstered his Magnum, the cold steel a small comfort against the overwhelming dread. He knew he couldn't take on Samson alone. He needed his team. He needed Ralph, his tech expert, whose gadgets could pierce the veil of the supernatural. He needed Venga, the scholar whose knowledge of ancient lore held the key to understanding Samson's power. And he needed Chet, the strongman whose brute force was as important as any weapon.

Mike slipped away from the alleyway, melting into the shadows of the city. The crimson stain of the fog lingered in his mind's eye, a constant reminder of the terrifying power he had just witnessed. He moved with a purpose that belied his exhaustion, his mind already strategizing, plotting, planning. The hunt was on, and this time, the stakes were higher than ever. This wasn't just about stopping a killer; it was about stopping a force of nature that threatened to consume Salt Lake City in a wave of crimson death.

The city, despite its outward facade of serenity, pulsed with an unseen energy, a network of ley lines that hummed beneath its streets. Mike felt this energy, a subtle vibration beneath his feet, a constant reminder that this battle extended beyond the physical realm. The fight wasn't just against Samson; it was against the city itself, against the ancient forces that had given birth to this nightmare. His mission was more profound than simply killing a vampire; it was a fight against the ancient darkness lurking beneath the surface of the seemingly peaceful city.

He reached his headquarters, a dilapidated garage converted into a fortress of technology and arcane knowledge. The air inside hummed with the low thrum of computers and the faint scent of ozone mingling with the earthy aroma of ancient artifacts. Ralph, his face illuminated by the glow of multiple computer screens, looked up as Mike entered, his eyes widening at the sight of his grim expression.

"I've seen him," Mike said, his voice rough. "Samson Bordeau. He's here, and he's unlike anything we've ever faced before."

Ralph's fingers flew across the keyboard, his movements precise, almost frantic. "Anything specific? Did you manage to get any readings? Any visual data?"

"Not much," Mike admitted. "The fog…it was strange. Sentient, somehow. And he moved...too fast. Too fluid. It was like watching a nightmare unfold."

The sound of footsteps echoed from the back of the garage. Venga entered, her face pale, her eyes reflecting the deep shadows of the workshop. She carried a worn leather-bound book, its pages filled with faded script and arcane symbols.

"I've been studying the old texts," Venga said, her voice barely a whisper. "There are legends, whispers…of beings capable of manipulating the city's energy, drawing power from its ley lines."

Mike nodded, his gut tightening. He knew what was coming. They were fighting something more than a monster. They were fighting something ancient, something that fed off the city's very essence. The hunt was on, and it was a battle they were likely ill-equipped to fight, a terrifying prospect made even more grim by the growing sense of dread settling upon the weary hunters. Their fight had just become immeasurably more dangerous. The stakes were now the very soul of Salt Lake City itself.

The meeting continued late into the night, fueled by caffeine, anxiety, and the growing weight of their grim task. As the first rays of dawn crept through the garage's grimy windows, a plan, rough and precarious as it was, began to take shape. They were far from ready, but they had to try. They had to find a way to stop Samson before he consumed the city, before he drained it dry, leaving behind only a hollow shell, a monument to his terrifying power.

The air hung thick with the scent of ozone and old leather, a strange perfume unique to their makeshift headquarters. It wasn't a glamorous operation; more a repurposed garage, its walls adorned with a bizarre tapestry of ancient weaponry and futuristic gadgets. This was where the unlikely alliance of vampire hunters coalesced, a blend of grit and genius forged in the crucible of countless battles.

Ralph, their tech expert, resembled a startled owl more than a seasoned warrior. His eyes, perpetually bloodshot from countless hours spent hunched over glowing screens, darted nervously from one monitor to another, a whirlwind of frantic keystrokes accompanying his every move. His arsenal wasn't comprised of silver stakes or holy water, but an array of customized weapons; EMF pulse rifles that could fry a vampire's nervous system, sonic disruptors that shattered their ethereal forms, and thermal imaging goggles that pierced the darkness, revealing the undead lurking in the shadows. He was the brains of the operation, the architect of their technological advantage, a man whose skills were as vital as any blade in their fight against the supernatural. He was the bridge between ancient lore and modern warfare.

Venga, a woman of contrasting extremes, was a whirlwind of contradictions. A petite scholar with a fierce intelligence, her slender frame betrayed the depth of her knowledge. She was a walking encyclopedia of occult lore, her mind a labyrinth of forgotten rituals, ancient prophecies, and the hidden histories of the supernatural world. Her arsenal was less tangible than Ralph's, but no less potent. She wielded the power of knowledge, the forgotten wisdom of centuries, decoding cryptic symbols, deciphering ancient texts, and interpreting the subtle whispers of the supernatural world. Her understanding of the ley lines crisscrossing Salt Lake City was crucial; without her knowledge, they would be blind men stumbling through a labyrinth of supernatural energy. She possessed the key to understanding Samson's power, and the potential weaknesses that might exploit it.

Then there was Chet. Where Ralph was cerebral and Venga was intellectual, Chet was pure, unadulterated muscle. A mountain of a man, his physique spoke of years spent honing his body into a weapon. He was the enforcer, the brute force that balanced out the team's more delicate talents. His weapons were as straightforward as his personality – a customized sledgehammer forged from blessed steel, and a set of brass knuckles imbued with holy symbols. His strength and unflinching resolve served as an anchor, a stark counterpoint to the technical sophistication of their other assets. He wouldn't be deciphering ancient texts or calibrating EMF rifles, but he would be the one holding the line, the one ensuring that their adversaries did not breach their defenses. He was the silent guardian, the unwavering wall that protected the rest of the team, his presence a potent deterrent against anything that dared to approach.

The garage itself was a testament to their eclectic approach. A mishmash of ancient relics and cutting-edge technology, it was a place where the past and present collided. Dust-covered tomes lay nestled beside state-of-the-art computers, their screens flickering with complex algorithms and encrypted data. Beside shelves crammed with silver-plated weaponry were racks filled with specialized EMF grenades and thermal-imaging devices. A chaotic harmony ruled this space, reflecting the unconventional nature of their enterprise, the delicate balance between ancient rituals and modern technology.

The night stretched on, the hours melting into a blur of intense discussion, punctuated by the hum of computers and the hushed whispers of strategy. Mike, weathered and scarred, laid out the details of his encounter with Samson, his voice low and grim. He described the crimson fog, its sentient nature, and the terrifying speed and grace of Samson himself. His words painted a vivid picture of a creature far more powerful and cunning than any they'd previously encountered.

Ralph, his fingers flying across the keyboard, painstakingly pieced together the scant visual data Mike had managed to gather. He analyzed the spectral readings, attempting to discern the nature of the fog, its composition, and its connection to the city's energy grid. He worked frantically, his concentration laser-focused, hoping to uncover clues that would give them an edge in the looming confrontation. He ran simulations, constructing mathematical models of Samson's movements, attempting to anticipate his next move. The data was incomplete, fragmentary, but it was all they had.

Venga, meanwhile, delved into the ancient texts, her eyes tracing the faded script, muttering incantations under her breath. She sought knowledge of Samson's origins, his weaknesses, his connection to the ley lines, anything that might give them an advantage. She unearthed fragmented myths and legends, whispers of an ancient entity capable of manipulating supernatural energies, feeding off the very lifeblood of the city. The texts spoke of rituals, of sacrifices, of a power older than the city itself. Her research was painstaking, tedious, but every piece of information she unearthed painted an even more disturbing picture of the enemy they faced.

Chet, ever silent, sat quietly, his gaze fixed on the maps of Salt Lake City laid out on the workbench. He listened intently, processing the information, formulating contingency plans, visualizing possible attack routes and escape strategies. His silence wasn't apathy; it was a form of intense concentration. He absorbed information not through words, but through observation, his mind a silent strategist, mapping out the battlefield, identifying vulnerabilities, and envisioning potential scenarios. He was the team's silent force, the physical embodiment of their last line of defense.

As dawn broke, painting the sky in hues of pale grey and muted orange, they had a plan. It was rudimentary, risky, and highly improbable, but it was all they had. They would use Ralph's technology to disrupt Samson's connection to the city's ley lines, Venga's knowledge to exploit his vulnerabilities, and Chet's strength to physically confront him. Mike would lead the charge, guided by his years of experience and a fierce determination to protect his city, even if it meant sacrificing everything. They were an unlikely alliance, a motley crew united by a shared purpose and a grim determination to face whatever darkness awaited them. The crimson fog loomed, a harbinger of impending doom, but they were ready to fight. They had assembled their team, and now, the war truly began.

The first clue came not from a spectral reading or an ancient text, but from a discarded cigarette butt, stained crimson. Ralph, his owl-like gaze magnified by his thermal goggles, spotted it nestled amongst the overflowing trash bins behind "Nutmeg's," a dive bar known more for its clientele than its cocktails. The butt, analyzed under Ralph's high-powered microscope, revealed traces of a rare blood type – AB negative – the same type drained from the victims found near the city's ley lines. It was a tiny breadcrumb, but for the hunters, it was a significant find.

The bar's interior was a haze of cigarette smoke, cheap beer, and the lingering scent of desperation. The air hung thick with the weight of unspoken secrets, the kind that clung to the shadows in places like this. Mike, his face obscured by the gloom, moved through the crowd like a wraith, his movements fluid and silent, a predator surveying its prey. He scanned the faces, searching for a flicker of recognition, a trace of the crimson fog's lingering presence. The patrons, a mix of lost souls and hardened criminals, gave him little attention. They were used to the shadows, to the whispers of the city's underbelly.

Venga, ever the scholar, consulted her worn leather-bound book, its pages filled with a chaotic jumble of symbols and cryptic notations. She'd deciphered a passage detailing a ritualistic sacrifice performed near a specific confluence of ley lines, a location surprisingly close to Nutmeg's. The ritual involved the draining of a rare blood type – AB negative. It was, she surmised, a ritual designed to empower Samson, fueling his connection to the city's energetic network.

The hunt continued, their path weaving through the labyrinthine streets of Salt Lake City. They moved from the neon-lit alleys of downtown, where the city's vibrant pulse throbbed with the energy of humanity, to the quiet solitude of forgotten cemeteries, where the city's past lay buried beneath layers of dust and crumbling stone. Each location offered a new piece of the puzzle, a new glimpse into Samson's movements.

They followed the trail of crimson stains to an abandoned warehouse district, its skeletal structures looming like skeletal fingers against the twilight sky. The air here was colder, heavier, charged with a strange, almost palpable energy. The faint smell of ozone, stronger here than anywhere else, hinted at a disruptive flow in the city's ley lines. Ralph's instruments shrieked with feedback, the overload a testament to the powerful energy emanating from the area, an energy that Samson was clearly manipulating.

Within the derelict warehouse, they found more evidence: a shattered altar, stained with the same crimson residue, and surrounding it, scattered runes etched into the concrete floor. Venga recognized them as a variation on the symbols she'd found in her ancient texts, suggesting a recent ritual. She carefully photographed the runes, her fingers tracing their faint outlines, trying to decipher their meaning, trying to understand the pattern of Samson's movements and ritualistic practices.

Their investigation of the warehouse revealed something far more disturbing than mere remnants of a ritual. Deep within the structure, concealed behind a false wall, they uncovered a network of tunnels – a subterranean labyrinth that ran beneath the city. The tunnels pulsed with the same unnatural energy that permeated the warehouse. Ralph's equipment went haywire, unable to properly measure the fluctuating energy levels. Venga's research confirmed that these tunnels were ancient, predating the city itself, acting as conduits for the city's ley lines, channeling the city's energy.

Following these subterranean passages, they found themselves deep beneath the city, far removed from the noise and chaos of the urban landscape above. The darkness here was oppressive, the air heavy and stale, the silence broken only by the rhythmic drip of water and the occasional tremor in the earth. The walls of the tunnels were damp and cold, slick with moisture, covered in a strange, phosphorescent fungus that cast an eerie glow.

The tunnels led them to an underground chamber, vast and cavernous, where the air vibrated with a potent energy. At the heart of the chamber, they discovered a massive crystal, pulsating with an unnatural light, its surface etched with intricate patterns. Venga immediately recognized it as a focus point for the city's ley lines, a nexus of power. She suspected that Samson was using this crystal as an anchor, drawing power from the city's energy grid to amplify his abilities. The crystal pulsed with a rhythm that seemed to mirror Samson's heartbeat.

As they were studying the crystal, a figure emerged from the shadows, the crimson fog swirling around him like a sentient shroud. Samson Bordeau, the fog-vampire, stood before them, his eyes burning with an unnatural intensity. His presence filled the chamber, suffocating them with his power. He spoke, his voice a chilling whisper that resonated in the vast chamber, "You have come so far, little hunters. But you will never understand the power I wield."

The ensuing confrontation was brutal and swift. Chet's sledgehammer met Samson's spectral form, but the blows seemed to pass right through him, his ethereal form shimmering and reforming. Ralph unleashed a barrage of EMF pulses, but Samson deflected them with a flick of his wrist, the energy crackling harmlessly around him. Venga, armed with nothing but her knowledge, chanted a counter-spell, attempting to disrupt the nexus of power, to sever Samson's connection to the ley lines.

The crystal pulsed faster, brighter, mirroring the intensity of the battle. The chamber shook, the ground trembling beneath their feet, as Samson's power surged through the tunnels, sending tremors through the city above. This battle was not just a fight against a single vampire; it was a battle for the very soul of Salt Lake City. The hunters knew that if Samson gained complete control of the ley lines, the city would be lost to his power, its life force drained away, leaving behind nothing but a desolate husk. The hunt had become a fight for survival, not just for themselves, but for the entire city. The fight for Salt Lake City had truly begun.

The air in the underground chamber crackled with the raw energy of the ley lines, a tangible hum that vibrated in their bones. Mike, ever the pragmatist, had positioned himself behind a crumbling pillar, his custom-built .454 Casull gleaming faintly in the dim light. He'd learned long ago that silver bullets were useless against creatures like Samson, but the sheer power of the round might still inflict some damage. He focused on the pulsing crystal, its eerie light illuminating the dust motes dancing in the air. This was it, the heart of Samson's power, the source of his unnatural strength.

Ralph, his tech whiz abilities now rendered nearly useless by the energy overload, worked frantically on his modified EMP device, cursing under his breath as the circuits sputtered and failed. The crystal's interference was overpowering, overwhelming his equipment. He tried to recalibrate, sweat beading on his brow, his fingers flying across the controls, but the energy field was too volatile, too strong. This wasn't just a matter of technical skill anymore, it was a struggle against a force of nature.

Venga, meanwhile, remained focused on the crystal, her eyes locked on its hypnotic pulse. She muttered incantations in a language lost to time, her voice a low, rhythmic chant that seemed to weave its way into the energy of the chamber, a counter-melody to the crystal's ominous hum. She was trying to disrupt the flow of energy, to weaken Samson's connection to the ley lines, to provide a momentary advantage to their team. The ancient words flowed from her lips, a desperate plea to the forces that governed this subterranean realm. She felt the power of the crystal push back, a tangible resistance against her ancient words.

Chet, ever the brute, stood ready with his sledgehammer, its head crafted from a rare meteorite, a weapon designed specifically to harm creatures of the night. He'd felt the raw power of the crystal as he descended into the chamber and it sent a shiver down his spine. This felt different, more than just a vampire, this was an elemental force bound to this place, this city. He felt a sense of dread, a premonition of impending danger unlike any he had ever experienced.

The plan was simple, brutally effective in theory: a coordinated attack designed to overwhelm Samson. Chet would create a distraction, a wave of raw force to overwhelm the vampire's senses. Mike would follow, using the opening to unleash a devastating barrage from his .454 Casull. Ralph's EMP device would then disrupt Samson's energy field, creating a window of vulnerability, allowing Venga to deliver the final blow, a potent spell designed to sever his connection to the ley lines. It was a high-risk strategy, requiring perfect timing and flawless execution.

Chet charged, his sledgehammer a blur of motion, letting out a roar that echoed through the cavernous chamber. Samson, caught off guard, reacted instantly, the crimson fog swirling around him, momentarily shielding him from the blow. The sledgehammer impacted, but instead of a solid thud, there was only a sound akin to passing through water, a ghostly resistance. Samson was stronger, faster, more resilient than they had anticipated. The initial assault did little to stop him.

Mike seized the opportunity, firing three shots in rapid succession, the rounds impacting Samson's chest. This time, the effect was more pronounced, causing a ripple in the fog, but the vampire simply recoiled, the fog coalescing again, the wounds appearing to heal as if by magic. The .454 Casull rounds inflicted a small delay but nothing incapacitating, his spectral body regenerating as if it possessed the ability to reverse time.

Ralph's EMP device finally fired, a surge of energy that illuminated the chamber with blinding white light, but Samson was prepared. He vanished, seemingly absorbed by the crystal itself, his form disappearing into the pulsating light. The energy surged, the tremors intensified, the entire chamber vibrating violently. The ground began to crumble beneath their feet, causing them to stumble and lose their footing.

Venga's incantation was cut short by the violent energy surge, her concentration broken, her spell unfinished. The chamber was overwhelmed by Samson's power; the crystal's glow intensified. It was a near miss, a close call. They'd gotten a glimpse of his power, but they hadn't been able to inflict any lasting damage. He was simply too powerful, too connected to the ley lines.

Samson reappeared, his eyes blazing with an unholy light, the crimson fog swirling around him like a malevolent storm. He laughed, a chilling sound that seemed to echo from the depths of hell itself. "Fools," he hissed, his voice a guttural rasp that resonated with the tremoring earth, "you cannot hope to defeat me. I am the city, and the city is mine." He vanished once more, leaving them in the shaking chamber amidst falling debris and the lingering scent of ozone and fear. The hunters were left shaken, defeated, but not broken. They had faced Samson Bordeau, the fog-vampire, and had survived. But the near miss had only served to underscore the true scale of the threat they faced, the terrifying power they were up against. The hunt continued. The fight for Salt Lake City was far from over. The hunters staggered out of the collapsing chamber, their mission now more desperate, more vital than ever. The escape had left them bruised and shaken but alive, and with a renewed sense of dread and determination. They knew, beyond any doubt, that their confrontation with Samson was only just beginning. The crimson fog had retreated, but the storm was far from over. The hunters were not only hunting a vampire, they were fighting against the very essence of Salt Lake City, its very life force. The fight for the city's survival had truly commenced. The near miss had only served to strengthen their resolve. They would not rest, they would not surrender. They would hunt Samson Bordeau, even to the ends of the earth, if necessary. The fate of Salt Lake City rested upon their weary shoulders.

The escape from the collapsing chamber had been a blur of adrenaline and terror. They emerged into the Salt Lake City night, the biting wind whipping at their faces, a stark contrast to the stifling heat of the subterranean chamber. The city lights, usually a comforting beacon, now seemed cold and indifferent, mirroring the hollow ache in their hearts. The silence, broken only by the distant wail of a siren, felt heavier than the dust coating their clothes. It was in that silence, amidst the wreckage of their failed ambush, that the full weight of their loss crashed down upon them.

Chet wasn't with them.

The realization struck Mike first, a cold fist clenching around his heart. He looked around, his eyes scanning the faces of his companions, searching for the comforting bulk of Chet, the ever-present reassurance of his unwavering loyalty. But Chet was gone. The silence screamed his absence. The memory of Chet's powerful roar, his reckless charge, his unwavering determination, replayed in Mike's mind, a painful echo in the chilling silence of the night.

Ralph, usually a whirlwind of frantic energy, stood frozen, his face ashen, his eyes wide with a mixture of shock and grief. His fingers, still trembling from the energy surge, unconsciously reached up to touch the burn marks that now marred his skin. The physical pain was nothing compared to the gut-wrenching sorrow that threatened to consume him. Chet had been more than just a teammate; he had been a brother, a confidant, a source of unwavering strength.

Venga, usually stoic and reserved, knelt on the cold concrete, her face buried in her hands. The ancient incantations she'd chanted seemed to have lost all meaning, their power extinguished by the brutal reality of Chet's death. The strength she'd drawn from the ancient lore felt hollow now, replaced by a raw, visceral grief. The weight of their shared losses, the burdens of their dangerous lives, pressed down upon her, threatening to crush her. She whispered Chet's name, a prayer lost in the unforgiving city night, a plea for solace in the face of unbearable sorrow.

Mike placed a hand on Ralph's shoulder, the gesture clumsy, inadequate in the face of such devastating loss. He didn't know what to say, words seemed cheap and hollow.

The reality of Chet's death hit him anew; he felt the crushing weight of responsibility, the burden of leadership, the knowledge that he had failed to protect one of his own. He had seen men die in this business, men lost to the horrors of the night, but Chet's death felt different. It was a personal betrayal, a violation of the unspoken bond that had held their team together.

The silence stretched, thick with unspoken sorrow, until Ralph finally spoke, his voice barely a whisper, choked with emotion. "He…he didn't even scream." The simple statement was devastating in its stark depiction of Chet's final moments, highlighting the swift, brutal nature of Samson's attack. The lack of a scream, the absence of a final struggle, painted a horrific image in their minds, a scene of silent, unimaginable pain.

Venga looked up, her eyes filled with unshed tears. "Samson...he didn't just kill him. He…he absorbed him." Her words hung in the air, a chilling revelation that added a new layer of horror to their loss. The thought of Chet's essence, his very being, being consumed by the fog-vampire, was a horrifying prospect, a violation that deepened their despair. The vampire wasn't just killing; he was assimilating, consuming, merging with his victims, their strength becoming his own.

Mike felt a surge of icy rage. The initial shock was giving way to an overwhelming, all-consuming anger. The near-miss in the chamber had been terrifying, but this—this was a personal affront. This was a violation, a transgression beyond all comprehension. He would hunt Samson with a ferocity they had never witnessed before, every fiber of his being consumed by a thirst for revenge that burned brighter than any vengeance he had ever known. He wanted him to suffer for what he had done, he would make sure of it.

Ralph nodded, the grief momentarily overshadowed by a similar surge of wrath. His usual technical expertise would be channeled into the hunt, focused on finding a way to finally vanquish Samson. He would transform his pain and grief into a weapon, his sorrow fueling his determination to make sure Chet's sacrifice would not be in vain.

Venga stood, her body stiff with sorrow and simmering fury. The ancient words she spoke now held a new weight, a new purpose. This was no longer just a hunt for survival; it was a sacred mission, a righteous war. She would use every ounce of her ancient knowledge, every whispered incantation, every ounce of her strength to destroy Samson.

The three survivors stood together, their grief binding them, their shared anger forging a stronger, more resolute bond. The loss of Chet had shattered them, but it had also tempered their resolve. The crimson fog had claimed one of their own, but it had also ignited a fire within them, a burning inferno of vengeance that would consume them until Samson Bordeau was dead. Salt Lake City had witnessed the fall of one of its protectors, but the fight for its soul would continue, fueled by the memory of their fallen comrade and the consuming fire of vengeance.

The night was cold, the city indifferent, but in their hearts, a chilling determination was born, a cold, hard resolve to hunt Samson with unparalleled brutality and cold, calculating precision. They would find him, they would corner him and they would extract their cold, deadly revenge for the loss of Chet, leaving a trail of Samson's life force in their path. Their shared mourning would not prevent them from making sure that Samson would pay for what he had done. The hunt wasn't just about saving the city anymore; it was about avenging Chet. It was about making sure his sacrifice wasn't in vain. The loss was immense, but the cost of inaction was far greater. The hunt would continue. The fight would continue. The vengeance would be swift and merciless. The city's fate, and their own, depended upon it. The memory of Chet's lifeless eyes, the absence of his comforting presence, would be their constant companion, the fuel that drove them through the long, dark nights ahead. The crimson fog had claimed a victim, but it had also awakened a force far more terrifying, a force fueled by grief, revenge, and the unshakeable loyalty of those left behind. The hunt for Samson had transformed; it was now a personal crusade, a holy war waged in the name of their fallen comrade.

The city's underbelly seemed alive, its shadows twisting and curling with secrets too dangerous to uncover. Venga crouched on the cold concrete, her whispered incantations trailing off into the night as her trembling hands clenched the earth. The ancient words she once wielded with unwavering conviction now felt powerless, crushed by the brutal reality of

Chet's death. Her voice cracked as she murmured his name, a plea swallowed by the biting wind, an aching prayer for a justice that felt agonizingly out of reach.

Chapter 2: Ley Lines and Lore

The biting wind continued its assault, whipping through the alleyways and across the desolate expanse of the Salt Lake City streets. The three remaining hunters huddled together, the shared grief a tangible thing between them, heavier than the oppressive silence of the night. Mike, his jaw clenched tight, ran a hand through his already disheveled hair, the weight of his loss and the responsibility of leadership pressing down on him. Ralph, his burns throbbing, checked his arsenal, the mechanical precision a stark contrast to the turmoil within him. Venga, however, remained apart, her gaze fixed on something unseen, her lips moving in a silent prayer or perhaps an incantation.

She clutched a worn leather-bound book, its pages brittle with age, the script within a chaotic dance of symbols and arcane words. This was no ordinary text; this was a grimoire, a collection of ancient lore passed down through generations of her family, a testament to centuries of battling the darkness. Within its pages lay the key, she hoped, to understanding Samson, to finding a way to defeat him. The book was heavy, weighted not just by its age and size, but by the weight of its secrets, the burden of knowledge it contained.

The pages felt cold beneath her fingertips, a chilling contrast to the heat that radiated from her own desperate search for answers. The flickering light of a nearby streetlamp cast long, dancing shadows, illuminating passages filled with cryptic symbols and faded illustrations. She traced the elegant cursive script with a trembling finger, deciphering the archaic language, each word unlocking a new piece of the puzzle. The text spoke of ley lines, of energetic pathways that crisscrossed the earth, channels of raw power that could amplify both good and evil. It described how these lines could be manipulated, their energies harnessed for incredible power, for both healing and destruction.

Salt Lake City, she realized with a growing sense of dread, was situated on a nexus of powerful ley lines. The city itself, unknowingly, acted as a conduit, a powerful amplifier for supernatural energies. The grimoire depicted intricate maps, star charts overlaid on geographical representations, revealing the intricate web of these unseen currents flowing beneath the city. The descriptions were vague, filled with symbolic language and metaphorical references that required deep understanding and interpretation. But as Venga delved deeper, a chilling truth began to emerge.

Samson's power, the sheer malevolence that radiated from him, was not merely his own. He was drawing upon the ley lines, feeding upon their energy, amplifying his abilities to a terrifying degree. The city itself was fueling the vampire, providing him with an almost limitless source of power. The more he fed, the stronger he became, his influence expanding with each victim he consumed. This explained his seemingly inexhaustible strength, his ability to heal rapidly, his terrifying resilience.

The realization struck her with the force of a physical blow. She traced a finger along a particularly detailed illustration depicting a swirling vortex of energy beneath the city's heart, resonating with the ley lines. The drawing was accompanied by a chilling description: "The Crimson Heart," it read, "where the earth bleeds, and shadows dance." The Crimson Heart, she realized with a shudder, was a location where the ley lines converged, a point of immense power, the very source of Samson's strength. It was located near Temple Square, the city's most sacred ground.

Venga's heart pounded in her chest. The discovery was both terrifying and empowering. Terrifying because it revealed the immense power Samson commanded, empowering because it offered a potential weakness. If they could disrupt the flow of energy to the Crimson Heart, they could cripple Samson, perhaps even destroy him. But disrupting a nexus of ley lines was no easy task. It required precise knowledge, intricate rituals, and a level of magical power that even she, with her deep understanding of ancient lore, felt uncertain she possessed.

She looked up, her eyes meeting the worried gazes of Mike and Ralph. The weight of her discovery hung heavy in the air, a palpable tension that mirrored the storm raging within her. She had to tell them, to share the burden of this knowledge, to forge a new strategy based on this terrifying truth. The initial shock gave way to a grim determination. They wouldn't rely solely on bullets and technology this time. This was a battle that transcended the mundane, a fight that required a combination of modern weaponry and ancient magic.

"I've found something," she announced, her voice low but firm, the years of battling shadows lending it a quiet strength. "Samson… he's not just a vampire. He's feeding off the city's ley lines. His power is amplified, magnified, by the energies running beneath our feet."

Mike exchanged a look with Ralph, his eyes reflecting a mixture of apprehension and grim determination. They both knew the implications of her discovery. The fight was no longer a simple matter of tracking and eliminating a powerful predator. It had become a battle against the very essence of the city, a struggle for its supernatural soul.

"And this Crimson Heart?" Ralph asked, his voice strained, his gaze fixed on the grimoire in Venga's hands. "Where is it?"

Venga pointed to a specific area on the city map depicted in the book. "Near Temple Square," she said, her voice barely above a whisper. "It's a nexus, a point of immense power. If we can disrupt the flow of energy there, we can weaken Samson, maybe even destroy him. But it's dangerous. Extremely dangerous." She paused, her eyes flickering, reflecting the gravity of the situation. "We need a plan. And we need to act fast."

The night held its breath, the city lights twinkling like distant stars in the inky blackness. The cold wind continued its relentless assault, but within the hearts of the three hunters, a new kind of fire was kindled – the fire of desperate hope, burning against the chilling reality of their predicament. Their previous attempts had been brute force, a head-on confrontation with a foe far too powerful. Now, they possessed a potential key, a strategic advantage. The Crimson Heart was their new target. The battle for Salt Lake City's soul would be waged in a realm far beyond the concrete jungle, in the unseen world of ley lines and ancient magic, a world where their fate, and the city's, hung precariously in the balance.

The next few hours were a blur of frantic activity. Ralph, despite his injuries, painstakingly reviewed satellite imagery, cross-referencing it with Venga's findings, attempting to pinpoint the exact location of the Crimson Heart. Mike, ever the pragmatist, coordinated their preparations, assembling their arsenal, combining cutting-edge technology with the ancient artifacts Venga had retrieved from her family's grimoire. Venga, meanwhile, poured over her ancient texts, seeking further insight, attempting to decipher the precise rituals necessary to disrupt the ley lines, to sever Samson's connection to the city's supernatural power source.

The air crackled with tension, the silence punctuated only by the rhythmic tapping of Ralph's keyboard, the whispered incantations of Venga, and the occasional grunts of Mike as he cautiously checked and re-checked their weaponry. The weight of their task was immense, the odds stacked against them, but a fierce determination shone in their eyes, a refusal to let Chet's sacrifice be in vain. They knew the risks; they understood the magnitude of their undertaking. But they were hunters, and this was their hunt. This time, however, the hunt was not merely about survival; it was about redemption, about avenging their fallen comrade, about saving the city from the heart of darkness that pulsed beneath its streets.

The hunt had evolved. It was no longer just about tracking down a aable vampire. It was about unraveling a mystical secret, about confronting a supernatural force that was far more pervasive and powerful than they could have ever imagined. The crimson fog had claimed one of their own, but in its wake, it had revealed a vulnerability, a hidden weakness that they would exploit, a secret they would wield to turn the tide of the war. The battle for Salt Lake City was far from over, but the tide was beginning to turn. The hunt for Samson Bordeau had become a desperate race against time, a fight for the city's soul, a battle fought in the realm between the mundane and the mystical, a struggle that would determine not only their survival, but the very fate of the city. The fight had begun.

Ralph, his face pale but his eyes burning with grim determination, hunched over his workbench. The makeshift lab, set up in the cramped basement of Mike's abandoned warehouse, hummed with a low, almost imperceptible thrum. Wires snaked across the cluttered surface, connecting a chaotic array of components: salvaged military-grade electronics, repurposed industrial capacitors, and strange, almost archaic components salvaged from Venga's family grimoire. The air was thick with the smell of ozone and burnt solder, a testament to the long, arduous hours Ralph had spent working since Venga's revelation.

He wasn't just a tech guy; he was an engineer, a tinkerer, a problem-solver. He thrived on challenges, and this – neutralizing a vampire who was drawing power from the city's ley lines – was the biggest challenge he'd ever faced. His usual toolkit of hacking and surveillance techniques were useless here. This required something different, something entirely new. Something that could interact with the supernatural, not just monitor it.

His fingers, nimble and precise, worked with the practiced ease of a surgeon. He soldered a tiny, intricately designed circuit board, its surface etched with patterns that resembled the diagrams from Venga's grimoire. This wasn't just a technological solution; it was a marriage of technology and ancient lore, a fusion of the mundane and the mystical. The device, which he had christened the "Ley Line Disruptor," was a complex interplay of frequencies, carefully calculated to resonate with the specific vibrational patterns of the city's ley lines.

The core component was a modified Tesla coil, capable of emitting highly focused bursts of electromagnetic energy. Ralph had painstakingly calibrated the coil's output to match the resonant frequency of the Crimson Heart, a frequency he'd painstakingly derived by analyzing the satellite imagery and comparing it to the cryptic symbols in Venga's book. The coil itself was housed within a Faraday cage, a protective shell designed to prevent the uncontrolled release of energy and protect the user from the potentially catastrophic consequences of tampering with forces beyond human comprehension. The cage itself wasn't entirely standard; Ralph had incorporated materials mentioned in the grimoire, specifically a rare type of obsidian found only in the remote mountains of Utah, believed by Venga to possess unique properties that could enhance the device's ability to interact with the ley lines.

Surrounding the Tesla coil were arrays of smaller, modified radio transmitters and receivers. These acted as sensors, constantly monitoring the energy flow of the ley lines, feeding real-time data back to the main processor. The processor, a custom-built unit incorporating military-grade encryption and fail-safes, analyzed the incoming data, adjusting the frequency and intensity of the Tesla coil's output to maintain optimal disruption of the energy flow without causing a catastrophic surge or unintended consequences. The entire system was powered by a series of high-capacity lithium-ion batteries, scavenged from decommissioned military drones, sufficient to provide several hours of continuous operation. The device was also equipped with a sophisticated cooling system to prevent overheating, a critical consideration given the immense power it was designed to handle.

The final piece was a small, hand-held control unit. This allowed Ralph to remotely control the Ley Line Disruptor, adjusting its parameters and monitoring its performance. The control unit had a clear OLED screen displaying key data – the current ley line activity, the power output of the Tesla coil, and the overall system status. An array of tactile buttons and a rotary dial provided precise control over the device's functionality. The whole device looked less like a scientific instrument and more like a piece of gothic steampunk artistry, a testament to Ralph's ability to seamlessly blend technology and arcane knowledge.

But the design wasn't merely about raw power; it was about precision. Disrupting the ley lines without causing unpredictable consequences was critical. A surge of uncontrolled energy could have devastating consequences, potentially causing earthquakes, power outages, or even creating rifts in reality. Ralph's design incorporated a complex feedback loop system, constantly monitoring the energy flow and adjusting the device's output to prevent such catastrophic scenarios. The obsidian components were crucial in this aspect; Ralph believed, based on Venga's information, that they acted as a kind of regulator, smoothing out the energy flow and preventing uncontrolled surges.

The process hadn't been without its setbacks. Ralph had experienced several near-misses, several close calls where the device nearly overloaded or malfunctioned. He'd worked tirelessly, fueled by adrenaline and black coffee, spending sleepless nights tinkering, testing, refining, until he'd finally achieved a level of stability that he deemed acceptable for deployment. He'd burned himself several times, suffered minor electrical shocks, and endured the constant nagging fear that he was working with forces far beyond his comprehension. Yet, he pressed on, driven by the need to avenge Chet and the desperate hope that he could save the city.

As he finished the final calibration, a wave of exhaustion washed over him. He leaned back, his eyes tracing the intricate network of wires and components, a tangible representation of his efforts, a testament to his skill and dedication. The Ley Line Disruptor, sleek and menacing, pulsed with a faint, internal hum, a low thrumming that echoed the unseen energies flowing beneath the city. It was a risky gamble, a leap of faith into the unknown. But it was their only chance. He knew the risks; he understood the potential consequences. But he had done everything he could. He had built his weapon. He had prepared for the fight. Now, they would fight. The fate of Salt Lake City, and perhaps much more, rested on this machine, on his shoulders, on the shoulders of his team. The hunt would continue, but now armed with a far more potent weapon than bullets and prayers. The fight was far from over, but the tide was beginning to shift in their favor.

The flickering fluorescent light of Mike's warehouse basement cast long, dancing shadows across the assembled hunters. Ralph, still buzzing with the adrenaline of his recent triumph, carefully placed the Ley Line Disruptor in a reinforced carrying case. The device, despite its steampunk aesthetic, hummed with a contained power that spoke of potent, untamed energy. Venga, her face etched with the weight of her family's legacy, traced the symbols on a worn leather-bound grimoire, her lips moving in a silent prayer or perhaps a muttered incantation. Mike, ever the pragmatist, surveyed the room with his sharp, calculating gaze. Chet's absence hung heavy in the air, a palpable void in their usually boisterous camaraderie.

"Alright," Mike began, his voice low and gravelly, the sound echoing in the cavernous space. "Ralph's done the impossible. He's given us a fighting chance. But this isn't a stroll in the park. Samson's drawing power from the ley lines, making him stronger, faster, harder to kill." He gestured to a large map of Salt Lake City spread across the workbench, its streets illuminated with glowing red lines representing the city's ley lines. Venga had thoughtfully mapped them, using a combination of her family's ancient texts and modern satellite imagery.

"The Crimson Heart," Venga whispered, her finger tracing the most intense red line that pulsed faintly at the city's center, "is the strongest point in the network. Samson feeds from it, using it as a conduit for power. Disrupting it is key, but it's a high-risk operation. A disruption could cause unforeseen consequences—

earthquakes, power surges..." Her voice trailed off, the weight of the potential catastrophe pressing heavily on her.

"Which is why we're not hitting the Crimson Heart directly," Mike interrupted, his voice sharp but controlled. "Ralph's device will create a localized disruption, weakening Samson. We'll hit him when he's vulnerable, but we need a plan to get close without getting turned into juice. Venga, what about the secondary ley lines? Can we use them to our advantage?"

Venga nodded, her eyes glowing with a grim intelligence. "The secondary lines are weaker, less concentrated. Samson uses them for replenishment, but he wouldn't rely on them as much as the Crimson Heart. We can use them as escape routes, potential ambush points. But we need to be precise." She tapped a location on the map, a deserted industrial zone just outside the downtown core. "The western spur intersects with an abandoned subway tunnel. We set up an ambush there. The tunnel is a blind spot on the ley line, less likely to cause him issues."

Ralph, ever the strategist, added his input. "The Ley Line Disruptor needs a clear line of sight to the Crimson

Heart. I'll position it on the top of the Bonneville Salt Flats Hotel, the highest point in this area. It will disrupt the flow, but only temporarily. We need to move quickly and decisively."

"What about Samson's speed?" Mike questioned. "He's incredibly fast. How do we even hope to get close?"

"Distraction," Venga suggested, her gaze sharp. "We create a diversion, something to draw his attention away from the tunnel. A flashbang or something bigger, perhaps?"

"We need something big enough to pull his attention away but small enough that it won't alert the city," Mike countered, considering. "A large-scale controlled power surge, localized to a specific area? Ralph?"

Ralph pondered. "I can do it. I can overload a section of the city grid, using a modified frequency disruptor to send a cascade of false surges. It would look like a major electrical blackout caused by an equipment failure, exactly the sort of chaos Samson would likely find hard to ignore. It will distract him."

"Good," Mike nodded. "We use the disruption as cover to get into the subway tunnel. Ralph will have the Ley Line Disruptor active. We'll use that western spur to hit him when his power is weakened. Venga, you'll be at the front, your family's techniques used to target him once the disruption starts. I'll use my specialized weaponry to create a supporting assault, aiming for the ley-line points embedded within him."

"And what's our retreat plan?" asked Ralph, already anticipating potential problems.

"We move through the tunnel, using the secondary lines as guides," Venga said. "The tunnel system extends far beneath the city. That will give us time to regroup."

Mike nodded. "This is a high-risk operation. One wrong move, one missed signal, and we're all dead. But we have a chance. We've got the technology, the lore, and the teamwork. We're ready."

The weight of their task pressed heavily upon them, the stark reality of the mission hanging in the air like a shroud. This wasn't just about killing a vampire; it was about protecting the city, about avenging Chet, about facing the terrifying unknown with courage and determination. The silence that followed Mike's words was a testament to the gravity of their undertaking, a profound understanding of the potential consequences and the courage required to press forward. The plan was bold, audacious, and potentially suicidal. But it was their only hope. The next few hours would determine not just their fate but the fate of Salt Lake City itself.

The hours passed slowly, punctuated by the methodical preparation for their assault. Ralph checked and rechecked his equipment, ensuring that every wire was connected, every setting calibrated to perfection. Venga performed her ritualistic preparations, chanting low incantations as she prepared ancient amulets and blessed weapons. Mike sharpened his stakes, delicately cleaning his specialized weaponry, and intricately testing the functions of each, running through a mental checklist of each piece of equipment. The tension in the warehouse was palpable, a thick, suffocating blanket of anticipation and apprehension.

As dawn approached, painting the sky in hues of grey and orange, they moved into position. The urban landscape of Salt Lake City, usually vibrant and bustling, lay shrouded in an eerie stillness, a stark contrast to the impending chaos they were about to unleash. The city lights twinkled, oblivious to the supernatural battle about to unfold in its shadowy underbelly. This was their battlefield – a city steeped in history, crisscrossed by ancient ley lines, now the stage for a desperate fight against a creature of unimaginable power. The fate of the city, and perhaps more, rested on their shoulders. They were prepared to face the darkness, ready to unleash their wrath upon the night. The hunt was far from over, but the final act was about to begin.

The air in the warehouse crackled with a nervous energy, a stark contrast to the methodical precision of their movements. Each hunter, a cog in a carefully constructed machine, performed their duties with a grim focus that belied the underlying fear. Ralph, his usually boisterous demeanor replaced with a grim determination, precisely calibrated the Ley Line Disruptor, his brow furrowed in concentration. The device, a Frankensteinian masterpiece of salvaged technology and arcane symbols, hummed with a low, ominous thrum, a tangible representation of the power they were about to unleash. He checked the power source, the intricate network of wires and circuits, a testament to his ingenuity and skill. One wrong move, one faulty connection, and their entire plan could crumble.

Venga, her face pale but resolute, quickly prepared her arsenal. She laid out ancient amulets, each imbued with centuries of protective magic, their intricate carvings glowing faintly under the dim light. These weren't mere trinkets; they were conduits of power, designed to shield them from the raw energy of the ley lines and to enhance their abilities in combat. Alongside these, she arranged a selection of weapons – sharpened stakes blessed with holy water, silver knives etched with protective runes, and a small, intricately woven pouch containing a potent mixture of herbs and powders. Each item was carefully chosen, each with a specific purpose in their deadly dance with the fog-vampire.

Mike, ever the pragmatist, oversaw the final preparations. He checked the ammunition for his specialized weapons, ensuring each round was primed and ready. These weren't ordinary bullets; they were designed to disrupt the ley line energy that coursed through Samson's body, weakening his strength and making him vulnerable. He also examined his specialized stakes, thoroughly sharpening them to razor sharpness, ensuring they could pierce Samson's unnatural defenses. His methodical approach belied a deep understanding of the enemy they faced and the lethal precision required to defeat him. He checked his comms, ensuring clear lines of communication with the team during the ambush. This was their final chance; there would be no second attempt.

The silence in the warehouse was broken only by the occasional clink of metal against metal, the low hum of the Ley Line Disruptor, and the soft whisper of Venga's incantations. The weight of their task hung heavy in the air, a palpable sense of foreboding that mirrored the dread they felt in their hearts. They were about to face a creature of immense power, a being that drew strength from the very fabric of the city itself. Their success depended not just on their skill and courage, but also on a sliver of luck – a fragile thing in a battle against the supernatural.

As the first rays of dawn touched the horizon, painting the sky with hues of grey and orange, the team began their preparations for departure. Ralph carefully loaded the Ley Line Disruptor into a reinforced carrying case, its ominous hum a constant reminder of the power contained within. Venga strapped on her amulets, their protective energy wrapping around her like a second skin. Mike checked his weapons one last time, his eyes sharp and calculating. Their movements were precise, efficient, almost mechanical, a testament to their years of training and the countless battles they had fought together.

The drive to their ambush location was tense and silent, the hum of the engine a counterpoint to the gnawing anxiety that clawed at their insides. The city, usually vibrant and bustling, was eerily quiet at this hour, its usual cacophony replaced by a stillness that only heightened the sense of foreboding. As they approached the abandoned industrial zone, the landscape grew increasingly desolate, the decaying buildings and rusting machinery a fitting backdrop for their impending confrontation.

They positioned themselves strategically, each member taking up their designated position. Ralph, with the Ley Line Disruptor, climbed to the rooftop of an abandoned factory building, the highest vantage point in the area. His task was crucial; it was the first strike in their carefully planned assault. Venga and Mike took up positions in the deserted subway tunnel, their hidden vantage point providing an element of surprise. The cold, damp air of the tunnel, thick with the smell of dust and decay, seemed to amplify the tension. They waited, their senses heightened, every nerve ending on edge.

The city above them throbbed with a life of its own, unaware of the battle unfolding beneath its streets. The distant sounds of traffic and the occasional distant siren seemed almost surreal, a jarring contrast to the stillness of their subterranean lair. Time seemed to slow, each second stretching into an eternity, filled with anticipation and a deep, unsettling fear. The weight of their mission pressed down on them, the fate of the city and their own lives hanging precariously in the balance.

The plan was intricate and daring, a risky gamble based on precise timing and flawless execution. One mistake, one missed calculation, could result in their demise. But they had come too far to turn back. They had lost Chet, and the memory of his sacrifice served as both a warning and an inspiration. They would not fail him. They would not fail the city.

Suddenly, Ralph's voice crackled over their comms, a low, urgent whisper. "Activating the disruptor." The hum of the device intensified, filling the tunnel with a low, resonant thrum. Simultaneously, Mike initiated the secondary power surge, overloading a section of the city's electrical grid. The lights in a large swathe of the downtown area flickered and died, plunging the city into darkness. The chaos was exactly what they had hoped for. It was time.

The first sign of Samson was a ripple in the air, a distortion of light and shadow. Then, a chilling presence filled the tunnel. The hunt was finally on, the final confrontation about to begin. Their preparation, their skills, their courage – all would be tested in the ensuing battle. The fight for Salt Lake City's soul had begun. The fate of the city rested on their blade and their will to prevail. The coming confrontation would be a brutal, desperate struggle for survival. The fight for the city would be their legacy.

The city swallowed them whole. One moment they were in the relative safety of the abandoned subway tunnel, the next, they were navigating the labyrinthine streets of Salt Lake City, under the cloak of a moonless night. The air hung heavy with the scent of exhaust fumes, damp concrete, and something else… something ancient and unsettling, a faint metallic tang that hinted at the fog-vampire's proximity. Mike, leading the way, moved with the silent grace of a predator, his movements fluid and economical. He navigated the shadowed alleys and deserted side streets with an intuitive familiarity, his knowledge of the city's underbelly a crucial asset in their clandestine pursuit.

Venga followed close behind, her senses acutely attuned to the subtle shifts in the air, the almost imperceptible vibrations that betrayed Samson's presence. The amulets around her neck pulsed faintly, resonating with the city's ley lines, a network of energy that Samson seemed to manipulate with chilling ease. The protective energies they provided were a comfort, but they couldn't mask the palpable dread that settled in her stomach. This wasn't just a hunt; it was an incursion into the heart of a supernatural entity's domain.

Ralph, carrying the still-humming Ley Line Disruptor, brought up the rear. The weight of the device, and the responsibility it represented, weighed heavily on him. He knew that their success depended not only on their combat skills but also on his ability to deploy the disruptor at the precise moment. One wrong move, one moment of hesitation, could mean the difference between victory and annihilation. The city's nocturnal pulse was a constant companion, a soundtrack to their stealthy advance; the distant rumble of a passing train, the screech of tires on wet pavement, the occasional bark of a stray dog – each sound a potential threat, each silence a pregnant pause.

They used the city itself as their shield, its shadows and dark corners providing cover from Samson's preternatural senses. They moved from rooftop to rooftop, their progress a silent dance across the city's skyline. The buildings, usually towering symbols of human ambition, became their battleground, their surfaces offering precarious handholds and concealed pathways. The cold night air whipped around them, carrying with it the city's whispers – the hushed anxieties of the sleeping inhabitants, the low hum of electrical currents beneath the streets, the faintest echo of Samson's predatory presence.

Salt Lake City, usually a vibrant, bustling metropolis, transformed into a sinister, labyrinthine landscape under the cover of darkness. The familiar streets and buildings took on a menacing aura, their shadows stretching and twisting into grotesque parodies of themselves. The faint glow of streetlights cast long, eerie shadows, blurring the line between reality and illusion. The city itself seemed to hold its breath, anticipating the impending conflict.

As they progressed deeper into the city's core, the feeling of unease intensified. The air grew colder, the shadows darker, the silence more profound. They were moving closer to the epicenter of Samson's power, to the heart of the ley line network that fueled his existence. The city's energy, normally a comforting hum, now felt discordant, a cacophony of supernatural forces at play. Venga felt a prickling sensation on her skin, a premonition of danger that intensified with each step. The amulets around her neck vibrated more strongly, their protective power strained by the proximity to the vampire's influence.

They moved with an almost supernatural synchronization, their movements guided by instinct and years of shared experience. They were not merely a team; they were a single, tightly knit unit, each member complementing the others' skills and compensating for their weaknesses. They were a force of nature, a living testament to the human spirit's resilience in the face of unimaginable terror. Yet, the constant awareness of their mortality hung over them, a stark contrast to their almost supernatural efficiency.

The city's nocturnal life, usually a source of chaos and noise, now seemed oddly quiet, as if the city itself were holding its breath, anticipating the coming battle. Only the wind whispered through the canyons between buildings, carrying with it the chilling premonition of what lay ahead. The very air hummed with an unnatural energy, a palpable tension that tightened the muscles in their necks and sent a chill down their spines. The city was not merely a backdrop to their hunt; it was a living entity, caught in the crossfire of a conflict far beyond human comprehension.

The rhythmic thud of their footsteps on rooftops, the occasional scrape of metal against metal, were the only sounds in the vast urban expanse. The quiet was oppressive, the silence punctuated only by the occasional distant siren or the faint rumble of traffic far below. But beneath the superficial calm, an undercurrent of unease pulsed, a chilling resonance that echoed the silent dread in their hearts. They were entering the vampire's territory, and the city itself seemed to be holding its breath, waiting for the inevitable clash.

The closer they got to Samson's lair, the more palpable the fog became, a chilling mist that clung to the buildings and seeped into the alleyways. It wasn't just a meteorological phenomenon; it was a manifestation of Samson's power, a tangible expression of the supernatural forces at play. This was not simply an urban setting; it had become a supernatural battleground, the city's very fabric woven into the fabric of the conflict. The hunters moved through this unnatural fog with increasing caution, their senses strained to their limits. Each shadow seemed to writhe and twist, each whisper of wind carried a chilling echo of Samson's presence.

They reached a point where the fog thickened, obscuring their vision almost completely. The air grew heavy, thick with the stench of decay and something else… something indescribably alien. They were close. Too close. The city lights seemed to dim further, the darkness intensifying, pressing down on them like a suffocating blanket. The sounds of the city receded, replaced by an unnerving silence, broken only by the soft hiss of the fog and the pounding of their hearts. The hunt was nearing its climax, the final confrontation looming. They were at the precipice of a desperate battle, the fate of the city hanging precariously in the balance. Their journey had led them from the cold concrete of a subway tunnel to this, the heart of a supernatural nightmare, the city itself a silent witness to their struggle against the fog-vampire.

The air thickened, and the battle was about to begin. The city held its breath.

Chapter 3: Rooftop Confrontation

The fog, thick as a shroud, swirled around them, obscuring the city lights into hazy halos. Above, the moon, a sliver of silver in the inky blackness, offered little solace. Below, the city sprawled, a concrete jungle teeming with unseen lives, oblivious to the supernatural battle unfolding above. Mike, his eyes narrowed, scanned the rooftop expanse. He'd chosen this location – a cluster of interconnected buildings near the city's center – precisely because of its complex layout; a perfect battleground for a desperate fight.

"He's here," Venga breathed, her voice barely a whisper above the wind's mournful howl. The amulets around her neck pulsed fiercely, a frantic rhythm mirroring the rapid beat of her heart. The city's ley lines throbbed with an unnatural energy, a tangible manifestation of Samson's power.

Suddenly, a figure materialized from the swirling fog, a silhouette against the pallid moonlight. Samson Bordeau. He stood poised, impossibly tall, his form vaguely human yet distinctly otherworldly. The fog seemed to coalesce around him, swirling and shifting, a living extension of his being. His eyes, burning embers in the gloom, locked onto them, a chilling promise in their depths.

The fight began with a silent, brutal efficiency. Mike, his customized combat knife glinting in the dim light, lunged forward, a blur of motion that aimed for the creature's throat. Samson reacted with inhuman speed, deflecting the blow with a fluid grace that belied his monstrous nature. Their clash echoed in the silent night, a symphony of metal on bone, a brutal dance of death played out against the backdrop of the slumbering city.

Ralph, his hands steady despite the adrenaline coursing through his veins, activated the Ley Line Disruptor. The device hummed ominously, a counterpoint to the clash of steel and flesh, its energy building, ready to disrupt the ley lines that empowered Samson. The air crackled with raw energy; a tangible tension that hung heavy in the air.

Venga, never one to shy from the fray, moved with a predatory grace, her movements precise and lethal. She utilized the city's architecture to her advantage, using the rooftops' edges and the buildings' structures to gain a strategic advantage. Her amulets glowed, casting an ethereal light that danced across her face, highlighting the grim determination in her eyes. Each movement was a calculated risk, a deadly ballet of precise strikes and cunning evasive maneuvers.

Samson, however, was a force of nature. His strength was inhuman, his speed beyond comprehension. He moved like a phantom, one moment here, the next gone, his movements a blur of motion that defied the laws of physics. He fought with the ferocity of a cornered beast, his blows imbued with unnatural power, each strike carrying the force of a battering ram. The fog swirled around him, a chaotic vortex of unnatural energy that protected him, adding an ethereal, frightening dimension to his already formidable presence.

The rooftop battle raged on. The combatants traded blows, their movements a blur of motion, a deadly choreography of strikes and parries. The sounds of their struggle – the clang of metal, the sickening thud of flesh on flesh – echoed through the silent city. The city itself seemed to hold its breath, witnessing the clash of supernatural might.

As the battle wore on, Chet's absence loomed large in their minds. The loss of their friend fueled their determination. Each blow landed with the weight of grief, the memory of Chet a constant spur to push harder, fight longer. They weren't just fighting for their lives; they were fighting for their fallen comrade, for the memory of their shared purpose.

The Ley Line Disruptor, a marvel of engineering and arcane knowledge, hummed with a power that felt both exhilarating and terrifying. Ralph, his knuckles white against the grip of the device, felt the thrumming energy resonate through his bones. It was a weapon forged in the crucible of desperation, a last-ditch effort against a foe beyond conventional means. He'd spent months perfecting it, pouring over ancient texts and schematics, collaborating with a team of specialists whose expertise stretched from quantum physics to forgotten rituals. The device, a sleek, obsidian obelisk, pulsed with inner light, its surface etched with cryptic symbols that seemed to writhe and shift in the dim light.

But even with its advanced technology, the disruptor was unpredictable. Its power was raw, untamed, a force that threatened to overwhelm its wielder as much as its target. The energy it harnessed was inherently unstable, a chaotic energy drawn from the very fabric of the city's ley lines. Ralph had anticipated challenges; he'd run countless simulations, tested its limits in controlled environments. But nothing could truly prepare him for the raw, visceral reality of unleashing it against a creature like Samson Bordeau.

As he aimed the disruptor, a wave of dizziness washed over him. The air crackled with a palpable energy, a tangible force that pressed against him, threatening to crush him. He braced himself, focusing on the task at hand, his mind a shield against the onslaught of chaotic energy. The amulets Venga wore pulsed in response, their light mirroring the disruptor's glow, offering a measure of protection against the device's wild energy.

The moment he activated the disruptor, a blinding flash engulfed the rooftop. It wasn't just light; it was a wave of pure, unadulterated energy that ripped through the night, a seismic shockwave that seemed to shake the very foundations of the city. The fog, Samson's protective shroud, recoiled, momentarily dissolving into thin wisps before reforming. The effect wasn't instantaneous annihilation; instead, it caused a chaotic disruption, a temporary fracturing of the ley lines that fueled Samson's power.

Samson roared, a sound that tore through the night, a primal scream of rage and pain. The disruption had weakened him, but it hadn't destroyed him. The fog, now thinned and erratic, swirled around him like a wounded beast, its movements less fluid, less controlled. He staggered, his movements no longer the graceful, fluid dance of before, but rather clumsy, jerky reactions born of pain and confusion. He was still terrifyingly strong, still impossibly fast, but the edge had been taken off his supernatural prowess. The disruptor had cracked his armor, but not broken it.

The unexpected side effect of the disruptor's blast was the unexpected surge of energy that arced outwards. It wasn't contained; it was a forceful explosion that momentarily overloaded the city's electrical grid. Streetlights flickered and died, plunging sections of the city into darkness. Alarms blared from distant buildings, a cacophony of sound that added to the already chaotic scene. Even the city's skyscrapers, usually stoic and imposing, seemed to shudder from the shockwave.

Mike, capitalizing on the disruption, moved with lethal precision. His knife, a wickedly curved blade forged from a rare, almost mythical metal, danced in the darkness. He avoided the errant bolts of energy flashing across the rooftops, his movements a testament to years of honed skills and instinct. Each strike was a calculated risk, a precise thrust aimed at Samson's exposed points, the places where the disruption had momentarily breached his defenses.

Venga, utilizing her knowledge of the city's architecture, used the shadows and the erratic energy pulses to her advantage. She moved with a predatory grace, a phantom weaving through the chaos, her movements almost imperceptible. She deflected stray energy pulses, using them to her advantage, creating momentary blind spots for Samson. Her amulets pulsed frantically, resonating with the erratic energy, acting as both a shield and a conduit for her own formidable powers.

Samson, despite his weakened state, fought back with a ferocity born of desperation. Each blow landed with the weight of a thousand tons, its force amplified by his residual supernatural strength. He was no longer the master of the rooftop; he was a cornered beast, lashing out blindly, fighting for survival. The disrupted ley lines throbbed around him, unstable and chaotic, mirroring the tumultuous battle raging within him.

The battle raged on, a brutal dance of death played out against the backdrop of a city plunged into chaos. The erratic energy pulses from the disruptor created unpredictable hazards, forcing the hunters to constantly adapt and improvise. The rooftop became a maelstrom of energy, steel, and flesh, a chaotic battleground where the lines between reality and the supernatural blurred.

Ralph, exhausted but resolute, attempted to recharge the disruptor, knowing that this was a finite weapon with a limited capacity. The device glowed with an uneven, unstable light, a testament to the strain it had endured. He knew that a second blast, even if successful, might risk catastrophic damage to the city. The line between victory and utter destruction hung precariously in the balance.

The fight climaxed with a final, desperate clash. Mike, his knife gleaming, found an opening, a momentary lapse in Samson's defenses, a fatal flaw exposed by the disrupted ley lines and his own relentless assault. He plunged his blade into Samson's heart, a single, decisive strike. The fog finally dissipated completely, revealing Samson's true form, a grotesque parody of humanity, contorted in agony. His body convulsed violently for a moment, before disintegrating into dust, scattering on the wind.

Silence descended, broken only by the distant sirens and the wind whistling through the gaps in the buildings. The hunters stood, battered and bruised, exhausted beyond measure. They had survived, but the victory came at a heavy price. The city lay partly in darkness, a testament to the unpredictable power of the technology they had used. The consequences of their triumph were far-reaching and uncertain, casting a long shadow over their hard-won victory. They had saved the city, but at what cost? The scars, both physical and emotional, served as a constant reminder of the night's events.

The silence following Samson's demise was deafening, a stark contrast to the maelstrom of energy and violence that had preceded it. The city's groaning sigh, a collective shudder from the strain of the disrupted ley lines, was almost palpable. Mike stood amidst the wreckage, his chest heaving, his body slick with sweat and blood—both his own and Samson's. The mythical metal of his knife, usually gleaming, was now dull, caked with the remnants of the vampire's decaying flesh. He'd delivered the killing blow, a precise strike to the heart, but the victory felt hollow, a pyrrhic triumph purchased with a currency far more precious than the city's electrical grid.

Ralph, his face etched with exhaustion and concern, rushed to Mike's side. The Ley Line Disruptor lay discarded, its obsidian surface cracked, its internal hum reduced to a faint whisper. He knelt, his hands instinctively reaching for Mike's wounds. "Mike, you're hurt," Ralph said, his voice strained with worry. "Badly."

Mike waved him off, a weak, shaky gesture. "I'm…fine," he rasped, the words catching in his throat. "Just…winded." He tried to stand straighter, but a sharp pain shot through his side, causing him to wince. Ralph noticed a dark, spreading stain on Mike's tunic, blooming outward from a gash near his ribs. It wasn't just blood; it pulsed with an unnatural, dark luminescence.

Venga, her normally vibrant eyes clouded with a grim determination, examined the wound. Her fingers, tipped with a faint otherworldly glow, traced the edge of the laceration. The air around her crackled subtly, a silent testament to the raw power she commanded. "He got you," she whispered, her voice barely audible above the city's low hum. "It's not just a normal wound."

The dark glow intensified, spreading rapidly. Mike gasped, clutching his side, his face paling dramatically. The pain intensified, a searing, unbearable agony. He stumbled back, his knees buckling. "It's…burning," he whispered, his voice laced with an agony that transcended physical pain. He was not merely injured;

he was being consumed, something dark and malevolent burrowing into his very essence.

Ralph's eyes widened in horror. He recognized the signs, the chilling evidence of a parasitic infection, a dark magic infused into Samson's fangs. It was a slow, agonizing death, a corruption of body and soul, a fate far worse than a simple mortal wound.

"Chet!" Ralph yelled, his voice sharp and desperate. Ralph, usually stoic and rational, was still shaken by the fight's ferocity. He hurried to their side, his eyes registering the gravity of the situation instantly.

The silence that followed was punctuated only by Mike's ragged breathing, a grim counterpoint to the distant wail of sirens. The three hunters huddled around Mike, acutely aware of the ticking clock, the inexorable spread of the dark magic. Each second seemed to stretch into an eternity as they faced the stark reality of their teammate's impending doom.

Venga, despite the despair, began to work. She didn't have a cure, nothing in her arsenal could completely neutralize the dark magic. But she could slow it, buy them some time, maybe enough time to find a desperate solution. She began a ritual, whispering ancient incantations, her nimble fingers weaving intricate patterns in the air, guiding the faint, otherworldly light emanating from her amulets. The light pulsed with a rhythmic cadence, its intensity growing, a tangible force battling against the darkness that was consuming Mike.

The ritual was a desperate gamble. The energy it consumed was immense, and it was drawing heavily on Venga's reserves. Her face was pale, beaded with perspiration, and her breathing was labored. She was sacrificing her own power, her very essence, to buy Mike a few precious moments.

Ralph watched helplessly, his grief and frustration a silent, tangible presence. He had always admired Mike's unwavering bravery, his unshakeable determination. He'd never imagined this, never pictured the brutal price of their victory. The city, bathed in the pale dawn light, seemed to mirror his despair—still recovering from the energy surges, it seemed to reflect the battle raging within their group.

Mike, meanwhile, was fighting his own battle, a silent, internal struggle against the encroaching darkness. He could feel the dark magic gnawing at his soul, corrupting his thoughts, twisting his essence. The searing pain was almost unbearable, yet his determination, his unwavering loyalty to his team, remained unbroken. He knew his chances were slim, yet he held on, his consciousness clinging to the edge of oblivion.

He focused on Ralph, remembering countless shared victories, moments of camaraderie, the unspoken bond between them. He remembered Venga's selfless sacrifice, the incredible power she was sacrificing to keep him alive. And then Chet, his quiet strength, his steadfast loyalty, his unwavering support. The faces of his friends, blurred by pain and encroaching darkness, fueled his will to fight, to cling to life, however tenuously.

The ritual reached its crescendo. Venga's amulets glowed with an incandescent light, a blinding radiance that momentarily pushed back the encroaching darkness. The dark magic, momentarily repulsed, retreated from Mike's wound, leaving a trail of blackened, charred flesh in its wake. The pain subsided, albeit slowly, replaced by a lingering numbness and weakness. But the victory was fleeting, a temporary reprieve.

As the light faded, the darkness returned, but now at a much slower pace. Venga collapsed, breathless and exhausted, her body drained of its energy. Mike, though still alive, knew his time was limited. The dark magic would return. He was scarred, changed, forever marked by his sacrifice. But his sacrifice had saved his friends, given them the chance to recover, to heal, to continue the fight against the darkness that still threatened their city. The rooftop, once a scene of intense battle, now served as a grim testament to the sacrifices made, a silent monument to the bonds of loyalty that had forged their unlikely alliance. The cost had been high, but the price had been paid, and the city had been saved, for now. The silence that descended was both a victory and a mournful lament. The sun rose, casting its golden rays on the scarred cityscape, a pale imitation of the hope that had once filled their hearts. The aftermath, however, was a harsh reminder of their loss. The victory had been earned at a terrible price; and the memory of that price would forever haunt them.

The rooftop, a jagged expanse of concrete and steel, lay strewn with the detritus of battle. Twisted metal, shattered glass, and the lingering scent of ozone hung heavy in the air. Mike, his body ravaged, his spirit bruised, leaned against a crumbling parapet, the city sprawling beneath him like a wounded beast. The adrenaline that had fueled the fight was fading, replaced by a bone-deep weariness that threatened to consume him. Even the rising sun, painting the eastern sky in hues of blood orange and bruised purple, offered little comfort. It was a victory, yes, but a victory stained with the bitter taste of loss and sacrifice.

Ralph, ever vigilant, carefully examined the Ley Line Disruptor, its obsidian surface cracked and scarred. He muttered to himself, running a gloved hand along the fissures. "The energy surge…it overloaded the system. But it did something more," he murmured, his eyes tracing the intricate network of runes etched into the device's surface. "It…it weakened him."

Venga, her face pale and drawn, her usually vibrant eyes dull with exhaustion, approached them. The ritual had cost her dearly, draining her reserves of mystical energy to a dangerous low. She moved with a deliberate slowness, each step measured and careful, as if her very bones ached. "The ley lines… they were his power source," she rasped, her voice barely above a whisper. "He drew strength from them, used them to amplify his abilities, to control the fog, to…to feed."

"So, disrupting the ley lines weakened him?" Mike asked, his voice laced with a mixture of relief and disbelief. He looked from Venga to Ralph, his usually stoic demeanor replaced by a look of dawning comprehension. The pieces of the puzzle were falling into place. They'd been so focused on defeating him directly, they hadn't considered the source of his unnatural power.

"Not just weakened him," Venga corrected, her voice gaining a little strength. "It… it exposed a vulnerability. A weakness. He couldn't maintain his power without the ley lines fully charged. The Disruptor didn't kill him, but it crippled him."

Ralph nodded, his eyes fixed on the damaged device. "The runes…they pulsed differently during the overload. They reacted to the disruption, like a feedback loop. It created a momentary surge of counter-energy, a disruption in the flow. It was as if… as if it reversed the process, drawing energy *from* him, instead of feeding it *to* him."

The revelation hung in the air, a heavy silence punctuated only by the distant sirens and the city's quiet breathing. It had been a close call, a dangerous gamble that could have easily cost them their lives. They had, through sheer luck and desperate courage, stumbled upon Samson's weakness, a kink in his formidable armor that they had exploited ruthlessly.

"But how did he connect to them? How did he draw power directly from the city's ley lines?" Mike questioned, his curiosity piqued. He'd always been the more practical member of the team, the one who preferred concrete evidence over mystical speculation. He needed to understand, to analyze, to dissect the phenomenon.

Venga closed her eyes, her brow furrowed in concentration. "Ancient lore speaks of rituals, of binding spells, of sacrifices…it requires a profound understanding of the ley lines, a connection that transcends mere knowledge. It's a mastery only achieved by the most powerful and ancient of vampires." She opened her eyes, her gaze distant and filled with a chilling understanding. "He was not just a fog-vampire; he was a master of the ley lines, a conduit for their power, a parasite feeding on the city's very life force."

The implications were staggering. Samson hadn't merely been a threat to individual lives; he posed an existential threat to the city itself. If he hadn't been stopped, the consequences could have been catastrophic. The city's energy grid, its infrastructure, its very essence could have been drained, leaving it a husk, a desiccated shell bereft of life.

The thought sent a shiver down Mike's spine. He looked at the city sprawling below, bathed in the pale light of the rising sun, and felt a wave of gratitude for their hard-won victory.

The cost had been steep, but they had averted a disaster of unimaginable proportions.

Ralph, meanwhile, was carefully examining the remains of Samson's body. The vampire hunter, a creature of both precision and pragmatism, approached the task with scientific detachment. His careful examination extended to Samson's clothing and surroundings, searching for clues, attempting to decipher the ritual the vampire had performed to bind himself to the ley lines. The subtle traces of arcane symbols, barely visible on the vampire's clothing, the residue of strange herbs and powders, provided tantalizing hints of the dark magic used to accomplish this dangerous feat.

"He used a combination of ancient runes and a ritual that involved the sacrifice of..." Ralph paused, his voice low, as he pointed to a small, intricately carved bone lying near the corpse. The bone was oddly familiar, a symbol he'd encountered in forgotten texts. "A raven's bone... it symbolizes the messenger, the conduit between the worlds. He used it to focus the energy."

"The raven...it always seemed an odd coincidence," Venga mused, a flicker of understanding dawning in her eyes. "He favored ravens, always had a flock following him during the night, almost as if they were his familiars. They were not just familiars, they were part of the ritual, integral to maintaining his connection to the ley lines. The birds were feeding on the same source of energy he was drawing from, creating a symbiotic relationship between him, his familiars and the city's ley lines."

"And what about the fog?" Mike questioned, always keen on understanding the mechanics of the supernatural phenomena they faced. "The fog he commanded… it seemed to be more than just atmospheric conditions, it was a weapon, a shield, an extension of his power."

"The fog was…a conduit," Venga explained. "A medium, a way to transport and focus the energy he drew from the ley lines. It was saturated with dark energy, making it more than just a mist. It was a weapon, a shield that protected him, and it facilitated his feeding. The fog was a constant extension of himself, and through it, he controlled not only the environment but also his prey. He could manipulate it, shape it, use it to drain victims without them ever fully realizing it."

As the sun climbed higher, casting a long shadow across the rooftop, the four hunters gathered their remaining equipment, examining and cataloging the recovered artifacts. Each item—a shard of obsidian, a fragment of a broken amulet, the raven bone—represented a piece of the puzzle, a fragment of Samson's power and its source. The battle was won, but the knowledge gained, the understanding of the true extent of Samson's power and his connection to the city's ley lines, was a crucial victory. The hunt was over, but the fight had just begun. The shadows still lurked, and the city, while spared from immediate destruction, still held within it the potential for even greater darkness. The team had won this battle, but their victory was bittersweet, bought at a terrible cost. The scars of this fight, both physical and emotional, would remain long after the fog had dissipated and the city had healed. The city's pulse had been stabilized, but the echoes of the battle, the lingering presence of the defeated vampire's dark energy, resonated within them all. The sun, rising majestically, was a symbol of hope, but the chilling memory of the confrontation served as a grim reminder of their vulnerability and the ongoing battle against the forces of darkness that threatened to engulf their city at any moment.

The city stretched out beneath them, a breathtaking panorama of steel and glass shimmering in the nascent sunlight. But for Mike, Ralph, and Venga, the beauty was lost in the bitter taste of victory. Mike, his left arm hanging limp and useless, leaned heavily against the crumbling parapet, the throbbing pain a constant reminder of the brutal fight. His ribs ached, his lungs burned, and the taste of blood, both his own and Samson's, lingered on his tongue. He stared at his trembling hand, the fingers still stained crimson, a testament to the ferocity of their encounter. The adrenaline had long since ebbed, leaving him drained, hollowed out, a husk of the man he had been only hours ago. The weight of the loss settled upon him, heavy and suffocating.

Ralph, his face grimy and streaked with blood, examined the Ley Line Disruptor once more. The obsidian surface, now marred by deep cracks, reflected the rising sun like a fractured mirror. He ran a gloved finger along the most prominent fissure, tracing its jagged path. The energy surge had been immense, a violent convulsion that had nearly destroyed the device, and nearly cost them all their lives. He felt a profound sense of exhaustion, a weariness that went beyond the physical. The strain of the ritual, the mental and emotional toll of facing Samson's power, had left him emotionally spent. He was a machine, precisely planning and executing their strategy, but even machines break down.

Venga stood apart, a silent sentinel draped in shadows, her face devoid of expression. The ritual had extracted a heavy price from her. Her eyes, usually pools of vibrant emerald, were dull, the light within dimmed, extinguished by the exertion of her mystical abilities. Each breath she took seemed to be a monumental effort, each movement labored and slow. She had felt the drain of her power, the unsettling emptiness within, a chilling premonition of her mortality. She had glimpsed the abyss during the battle, the terrifying fragility of life, and the chilling reality of her own limitations. She trembled, not from cold, but from the lingering effects of the potent energies she had manipulated.

The rooftop was a battlefield, a testament to the destructive power they had faced. Twisted metal and shattered glass littered the concrete, a grim mosaic of their desperate struggle. The scent of ozone hung heavy in the air, acrid and sharp, a lingering reminder of the unleashed energies. It was a victory born of desperation, skill, and a chilling amount of luck, the kind of luck that left them questioning their survival, wondering if they had merely escaped death's grasp by a hair's breadth. The cost, however, was etched indelibly into their minds and bodies.

Mike reached out a trembling hand, touching the cold, lifeless form of their fallen comrade. The raw pain of their loss, so immediate and visceral, tore at his composure. Tears welled in his eyes, blurring the already indistinct outline of the city. It was more than just grief, it was the crushing weight of responsibility, the guilt of survival. They had fought as a unit, and now, one was gone. He felt the absence keenly, a hole ripped into the fabric of their team, a void that would never be truly filled.

The silent acknowledgment of their shared trauma hung heavy in the air. They had faced a monster, and they had defeated it, yet they all stood wounded, not just physically, but spiritually as well. The victory was a pyrrhic one, purchased with blood and sacrifice, a harsh lesson in the brutal reality of their profession. The city, sprawling beneath them, a canvas of light and shadow, seemed to hold its breath, as if in silent appreciation for their victory.

Ralph continued his analysis of the ley lines. The disruption had been significant, leaving a noticeable ripple in the city's energy flow. He could feel the residual energy, a phantom echo of Samson's power, subtly altering the city's pulse. It was a delicate balance, the city hanging precariously between stability and chaos. They had pushed the boundaries of their abilities, dangerously close to causing irreparable damage to the city itself, a terrifying prospect that made their success feel both hollow and incomplete.

Venga's mystic senses were still heightened, her awareness of the city's energy field acutely sensitive. She felt the lingering echoes of the battle, dark tendrils of energy that clung to the rooftop, refusing to dissipate. The energy, thick and oppressive, resonated with a chilling familiarity. It was a potent reminder of the darkness they had fought, a palpable trace of Samson's essence lingering like a malignant stain. She could sense the city's vulnerability, its precarious balance, hanging by a thread. The city had been saved, but it remained fragile, vulnerable to further attacks.

Ralph began to gather their scattered equipment, his actions a testament to his commitment. He checked the Ley Line Disruptor, its internal workings irrevocably damaged. It was a tool that had saved the city, but it was also a testament to the destructive force they had unleashed. It was a potent symbol of their victory and a poignant reminder of the precarious balance between creation and destruction, a subtle reminder that even in triumph, they walked a razor's edge.

The silence on the rooftop was broken only by the distant wail of a siren, a somber soundtrack to their victory. The rising sun cast long, stretching shadows, mirroring the shadows that had been cast into their hearts. The victory was palpable, but it tasted like ash. They had saved the city, yes, but the scars of battle remained, a vivid reminder of the losses sustained and the ongoing struggle against the unseen forces of darkness. The physical wounds would heal, perhaps, but the emotional scars, the memory of their comrade, the harrowing near-misses, would forever be etched into their souls, a testament to their sacrifice. Their pyrrhic victory was a stark reminder of their mortality, of the fragility of life, and the ever-present threat that lurked just beyond the veil of reality. The city might be safe for now, but the fight against the darkness was far from over. The hunters stood on the edge of a new dawn, victorious but weary, their future uncertain, their victory bittersweet. The shadows still lurked, and the fight had only just begun.

Chapter 4: Aftermath and Reflection

The dawn painted the Salt Lake City skyline in hues of bruised purple and sickly yellow, a stark contrast to the vibrant, optimistic image usually projected by its gleaming towers. From their vantage point, the hunters could see the extent of the damage, a tapestry woven from shattered glass, twisted metal, and the lingering scent of ozone – a battlefield carved into the heart of the city. The opulent skyscrapers, symbols of progress and prosperity, now bore the scars of a brutal nocturnal war. Scratched facades, pockmarked by energy blasts and vampire claws, stood as silent witnesses to the night's chaos. Below, the streets, usually teeming with life, were eerily quiet, the aftermath of the conflict casting a long, unsettling shadow. The city was breathing again, but it was a shallow, ragged breath, its rhythm still punctuated by the lingering echoes of the battle.

The rooftop itself was a desolate landscape. Debris from the confrontation lay scattered like the remnants of a macabre feast: chunks of concrete, shredded cabling, and fragments of the Ley Line Disruptor, all bearing witness to the ferocity of the fight. The obsidian shards, scattered across the concrete, glittered like malevolent eyes, reflecting the rising sun in fractured, distorted images. Each broken piece was a testament to the energy unleashed, the raw power they had channeled, and the risks they had taken. The air crackled with residual energy, a tangible reminder of the close call, the near catastrophic failure of their plan.

Mike, his good arm wrapped tightly around his injured left, surveyed the scene with a weary gaze. The physical pain was intense, a symphony of throbbing aches and burning muscles, but it paled in comparison to the weight of emotional exhaustion. He picked up a twisted piece of metal, its surface still warm from the energy surges. It was cold to the touch now, yet the heat of the battle still lingered in his memory, a searing brand on his soul. He ran his fingers along the jagged edge, feeling the metallic sharpness against his skin, a physical echo of the deep cuts that laced his own body. Each scar, physical and emotional, was a stark reminder of the night's brutal dance with death.

Ralph, his usually sharp eyes clouded with fatigue, knelt beside a shattered section of the parapet. He examined the fractures in the concrete, tracing the patterns with a gloved finger, his mind trying to piece together the events of the night, to analyze the flow of energy, to understand how close they had come to utter annihilation. He could feel the tremors in the city's energy field, subtle but palpable shifts in the ley lines, a delicate balance teetering on the precipice of chaos. His thoroughly planned strategy, usually a source of unwavering confidence, now felt fragile, vulnerable, a testament to the unpredictable nature of their adversary. The near-miss had exposed the limitations of their technology, the precarious balance between their power and the raw force of ancient evil.

Venga, her face pale and drawn, stood silently, her eyes fixed on the eastern horizon. The draining ritual had left her depleted, hollowed out, leaving her with a haunting awareness of her own mortality. She felt the lingering echoes of Samson's power, a dark stain on the city's energy field, a malignant influence that refused to dissipate. Her mystical senses were still heightened, her awareness painfully acute. She could sense the city's vulnerability, its fragile resilience, its precarious grip on stability. The victory was bittersweet; the city was safe, for now, but its scars ran deep, mirroring the wounds in her own soul.

Ralph, the pragmatist, began methodically gathering the remains of their equipment. Each item was a stark reminder of their near defeat, a testament to the brutal reality of their profession. The heat of the battle had left the metal components scorching, but they cooled quickly in the morning air. He handled each piece with care, storing them in his battered satchel, each item a symbol of both their strength and their vulnerability. His silence was heavy, a quiet acknowledgement of their shared trauma, their collective loss. He examined the damaged Ley Line Disruptor, a potent symbol of their success and their peril, a physical manifestation of their success, and the fragility of their victory. The city might be safe, but the battle had left deep scars, and they were far from being out of the woods.

The city below stirred slowly to life, the sounds of the awakening metropolis slowly filtering up to the rooftop. Sirens wailed in the distance, a mournful counterpoint to the rising sun. The sounds of traffic, the distant rumble of trains, and the murmurs of awakening city dwellers blended together into a symphony of urban life. Yet, for the hunters, the city's sounds were muffled, dulled by their exhaustion and the shadow of their shared loss. The physical wounds were painful, undeniable. But deeper than any physical ache were the psychic scars, the intangible wounds etched onto their souls.

The scars of the battle were not confined to the city's physical landscape. The emotional wounds were deeper, more pervasive, leaving an enduring mark on the hunters' psyche. The death of their comrade hung heavily in the air, a silent presence that permeated everything. They had fought as a unit, a brotherhood forged in the crucible of battle, and now, that brotherhood was irrevocably broken. The laughter, camaraderie, and inside jokes that once filled their missions were replaced by a haunting silence, punctuated by moments of intense grief and unspoken anxieties.

The cityscape, once a source of inspiration and a symbol of resilience, was now viewed through the lens of their shared trauma. The skyscrapers, once emblems of progress, now appeared as cold, uncaring giants, indifferent to their struggles. The familiar streets, once paths of adventure, were now a maze of memories, a landscape filled with the ghostly echoes of their fallen comrade. The city itself seemed to hold its breath, as if in silent mourning for the sacrifice made to protect its citizens.

Mike looked towards the east, where the sun was slowly climbing above the horizon. The light, though life-giving, felt cold and harsh, exposing the raw wounds of their victory. He thought of their fallen comrade, the vibrant life extinguished in the bloody chaos of the battle. The guilt gnawed at him, a persistent, unwelcome guest. He had survived, but at what cost? The question hung in the air, unanswered, heavy as a tombstone.

Ralph continued his silent examination of the ley lines, his mind attempting to process the complex energy shifts that had occurred. The disruption was more significant than he had initially feared. The city's energetic pulse was weakened, its resilience shaken. He realized that their victory was a precarious one, a fragile truce secured on the edge of a knife. The city was safe for now, but the underlying instability remained, a constant reminder of their vulnerability.

Venga felt the lingering echoes of Samson's power clinging to the rooftop, a malevolent presence woven into the fabric of the city. It was a chilling reminder that darkness could linger, unseen, lurking beneath the surface of normalcy. She could sense the city's trembling vulnerability, its susceptibility to further attacks, a constant threat hanging over its inhabitants. The victory was a temporary respite, a fragile moment in an ongoing battle.

Ralph, ever the pragmatist, began to prepare for their departure. He carefully stowed away their equipment, his movements methodical and precise. The silence was broken only by the occasional clink of metal, the subtle sounds of his preparations acting as a quiet counterpoint to the city's slow awakening. He surveyed the damage one last time, his face etched with a profound sense of weariness. The fight was over, but the aftermath would linger, a constant reminder of the sacrifices made and the battles yet to come.

As they descended from the rooftop, the hunters carried with them not only the physical scars of battle but also the weight of their shared experience. The city stretched below them, a breathtaking panorama of steel and glass, but its beauty was marred by the shadows of their hard-won victory. The city had been saved, but its scars mirrored their own. The battle was over, but the fight, the relentless, ongoing struggle against the unseen forces of darkness, had only just begun. The hunters, weary but resolute, stepped into the new dawn, their victory shadowed by loss, their future uncertain, their steps heavy with the weight of their shared trauma.

The descent was a slow, agonizing process. Each step down the fire escape felt like a betrayal, a surrender to the gravity that had so brutally grounded them after their aerial battle. Mike's left arm, a mangled mess of broken bone and shredded muscle, throbbed with a dull, persistent ache that resonated deep within his bones. The pain was a constant companion, a physical manifestation of the emotional turmoil raging within him. He'd survived, but the victory tasted like ash in his mouth.

He hadn't realized the extent of his injuries until the adrenaline faded, leaving behind a chilling emptiness. The raw wounds were a gruesome testament to the ferocity of the fight, a stark reminder of his own mortality. Each ragged tear in his skin, each searing burn, whispered a story of near-death experiences, a harrowing narrative etched onto his flesh. The medical team at the hospital had worked tirelessly, patching him up, but beneath the bandages, the pain remained raw, unyielding.

But the physical pain, though excruciating, was secondary to the emotional wounds. The death of Chet, his friend, his brother in arms, hung heavy in the air, a suffocating presence that invaded his every waking moment. Chet's laughter, his easy camaraderie, his unwavering pragmatism – all of it was gone, replaced by a gaping void that echoed the hollowness within Mike himself. He replayed the final moments in his mind, a grim, repetitive loop of violence and despair. Chet's fall, the desperate look in his eyes, the final, silent scream—it was a nightmare that refused to relinquish its grip.

Sleep offered little respite. When he did manage to drift into a troubled slumber, he was haunted by visions of the battle. The crimson glow of Samson's eyes, the chilling shriek as the fog-vampire lunged, the desperate struggle, the agonizing finality of Chet's death – it was a torment that extended far beyond the confines of reality. He would wake in a cold sweat, his heart pounding like a frantic drum, the taste of fear acrid on his tongue.

During his waking hours, Mike found himself retreating into a shell of his former self. The once-confident, jovial hunter was now a shadow of his former self, a haunted figure consumed by grief and guilt. He found solace in the quiet solitude of his small apartment, surrounded by the familiar comfort of old photographs and cherished memories. He'd lost more than just a comrade; he'd lost a part of himself.

The city, once his hunting ground, his playground, now felt like a tomb. The vibrant energy that once thrummed through its streets, the sense of boundless possibility, was replaced by a chilling stillness, a ghostly reminder of Chet's absence. Even the sounds of the city – the honking cars, the distant sirens, the murmur of voices – now held a morbid undertone, each noise a poignant echo of a life lost. He tried to resume his routine, to pick up the pieces, but each attempt felt like a desperate grasp at a fading hope.

Ralph and Venga tried to reach out, their efforts sincere, but their attempts at comfort fell short. Their words, though kind, felt hollow, unable to bridge the chasm of grief that separated them. They had shared the experience, the trauma, the victory; yet, they experienced it differently. Their losses were different, their wounds varied, and their attempts to understand the depth of Mike's despair proved futile. They could see the pain, they could feel the loss, but the experience remained profoundly isolating.

One evening, while staring out at the city lights from his apartment window, a single tear traced a slow path down

Mike's weathered cheek. He had always prided himself on his resilience, his ability to withstand the horrors they faced, but this loss was different. It was a blow that pierced the armor he had so delicately crafted, exposing his raw vulnerability. He felt stripped bare, exposed to the relentless onslaught of his grief.

The silence in his apartment pressed down on him, heavy and suffocating. He picked up a worn photograph of the team, a snapshot taken during a rare moment of levity. Chet's smile was radiant, his eyes sparkling with mischievous energy. The memory was a sharp, painful stab, a reminder of everything he had lost. He clutched the photo tightly, his knuckles white, and let the tears flow freely, finally allowing himself to fully embrace the weight of his sorrow.

He spent weeks wrestling with his demons, battling the waves of grief that threatened to drown him. He sought solace in long, solitary walks, allowing the city's rhythm to soothe his troubled mind, hoping to find a semblance of peace amid the chaos. He found himself drawn to the quiet corners of the city, the forgotten alleys and hidden parks, searching for a connection to something beyond his pain, searching for a way to honor Chet's memory.

Gradually, through the fog of his grief, a spark of resilience began to flicker. He realized that wallowing in his sorrow wasn't an option. Chet wouldn't want him to collapse; he would want him to carry on, to honor his memory by continuing the fight. The city still needed protecting, and he still had a role to play. He couldn't bring Chet back, but he could use this loss as fuel, transforming his grief into a driving force.

The process was slow, agonizingly gradual. It wasn't a simple resolution, but rather a subtle shift in perspective, a slow healing process. He started by visiting Chet's family, sharing stories, offering comfort, finding a strange solace in their shared grief. He began to accept that healing wasn't about erasing the pain but about learning to live with it, to integrate it into the fabric of his being. The memories of Chet wouldn't disappear, but they would no longer define him. He would honor his friend by living a life worthy of Chet's sacrifice, a life dedicated to the fight against the darkness that still threatened their city. He would keep fighting, not just for himself, but for Chet, for the memory of the comrade he had lost, for the city he had sworn to protect. The scars remained, both physical and emotional, but they were now badges of honor, testaments to the battles fought and the battles yet to come. The sunrise, once a stark reminder of loss, now represented a new beginning, a chance to rebuild, to heal, and to continue the fight against the encroaching darkness. The journey was long, arduous, and uncertain, but Mike, bearing the weight of his trauma and loss, knew he had to continue walking. He had to keep fighting. He had to honor his friend.

The sterile scent of antiseptic couldn't mask the metallic tang of blood clinging to the air in the hospital waiting room. Ralph sat stiffly, his gaze fixed on the polished floor, the rhythmic ticking of the clock a relentless counterpoint to the turmoil inside him. He hadn't slept properly since Chet's fall, the image of his friend's lifeless body a recurring nightmare that clawed at his sleep, replacing it with a fractured, unsettling rest filled with fragments of the battle – the screams, the fog, the searing pain. He could still feel the phantom weight of Chet's hand on his shoulder, the reassuring pressure a cruel mockery of his absence.

The guilt was a physical thing, a lead weight pressing down on his chest, suffocating him. He replayed the final moments again and again, dissecting every action, every decision, searching for a way to rewrite the ending. He should have been faster, stronger, more alert. He should have been there to catch Chet, to shield him from the vampire's attack. The thought gnawed at him relentlessly, a relentless self-flagellation that offered no solace, only deepening despair.

He'd been so close to Samson, so focused on securing the kill, that he'd momentarily lost sight of Chet. That fraction of a second, that blink of an eye, had been enough. Enough to cost Chet his life. Enough to shatter the fragile unity of their team. Enough to leave Ralph drowning in a sea of self-recrimination. He hadn't just lost a friend; he had failed him. The weight of that failure was crushing.

Venga's presence beside him was a quiet comfort, yet her attempts at consolation fell short. Her own wounds, both physical and emotional, were significant, but they weren't the same as his. She'd lost a comrade, yes, but she hadn't failed him. She hadn't been responsible for his death. Her grief was a shared sorrow, but Ralph's was a private hell, fueled by guilt and the relentless torment of "what ifs."

He tried to speak, to articulate the crushing weight of his remorse, but the words caught in his throat, choked by the rising tide of emotion. He clenched his fists, his knuckles white, his jaw tight, a silent testament to the inner battle raging within him. The silence stretched, thick and heavy, punctuated only by the muted sounds of the hospital – the hushed whispers of nurses, the distant beep of heart monitors, the muffled cries from other rooms, each a morbid counterpoint to his inner turmoil.

He thought of Chet's family, the crushing blow their loss must represent, the void left in their lives. The thought amplified his guilt, adding another layer to the burden he already carried. He owed them more than just his condolences. He owed them justice, even though he knew justice wouldn't bring Chet back. He couldn't offer them closure, but he could dedicate his remaining life to ensuring no one else suffered the same fate.

Days bled into weeks, the physical healing process slower than the emotional one. Ralph's physical wounds were superficial compared to Mike's, but the internal scars were just as profound, perhaps even deeper. He found himself isolating, withdrawing from the others, retreating into a self-imposed exile, haunted by visions of Chet's final moments. The city, once a familiar backdrop to their hunts, now felt alien, every corner a reminder of their shared past, a constant assault on his frayed nerves.

He found solace only in the rhythmic thump of his fists against the heavy bag in his makeshift gym, the sweat and exertion a temporary reprieve from the relentless tide of his guilt. Each punch was a release, a desperate attempt to exorcise the demons that haunted him. The pain, both physical and emotional, was a constant companion, a harsh reminder of the price of their victory.

Mike's attempts to reach out were met with a defensive silence. He understood Ralph's guilt, he shared it in his own way, but their grief manifested differently. Mike's sorrow was a consuming fire, a relentless inferno; Ralph's was a slow, suffocating weight, a burden he carried alone, unwilling to share the darkness that consumed him. He didn't want pity; he wanted absolution, a forgiveness he knew he couldn't grant himself.

He revisited the scene of the battle countless times, his mind replaying the events, searching for a way to alter the outcome. He'd examined every detail, analyzed every choice, only to be met with the same crushing reality – his failure had cost Chet his life. The knowledge hung heavy, a suffocating shroud that he couldn't escape.

Sleep offered little respite. His dreams were a kaleidoscope of fragmented images – Chet's terrified eyes, the chilling shriek of the vampire, the sickening thud of his body hitting the concrete below. He would wake with a gasp, his heart pounding in his chest, the cold sweat clinging to his skin. The nightmares were relentless, a relentless reminder of his guilt, a constant punishment for his failure.

The silence in his apartment was deafening, broken only by the occasional tick of the clock, the hum of the refrigerator, each sound a stark reminder of his isolation. He'd lost more than just a friend; he'd lost his faith in himself, his belief in his abilities. He was no longer the confident, unwavering hunter he'd once been; he was a broken man, haunted by the ghost of his guilt.

The burden was almost too much to bear, a crushing weight that threatened to drag him under. Yet, somewhere deep inside, a spark of defiance flickered, a stubborn refusal to surrender to despair. He couldn't bring Chet back, but he could honor his memory. He could dedicate himself to ensuring that Chet's sacrifice wouldn't be in vain. He could continue the fight, not just for revenge, but for the safety of the city, for the memory of his fallen comrade. He would transform his guilt into a driving force, fueling his resolve to hunt down every creature of darkness that dared threaten the innocent. The fight wasn't over; it had just begun. And Ralph, despite his guilt, despite his grief, would continue to fight. He had to. He owed it to Chet.

The rhythmic beeping of the heart monitor was a counterpoint to the erratic rhythm of Venga's own heart. She sat beside Ralph, his grief a palpable presence in the sterile hospital room, a stark contrast to the antiseptic smell. His silence was a wall, impenetrable and heavy with unspoken remorse. She understood; she felt the weight of Chet's loss just as keenly, but her sorrow manifested differently. Where Ralph was consumed by self-blame, a crushing weight of guilt, hers was a burning ember of resolve, a fierce determination to make sense of their loss, to find some meaning in the chaos.

While Ralph wrestled with his personal demons, a different kind of battle raged within Venga. The loss of Chet had shaken her to her core, but it hadn't broken her. The raw pain, the visceral shock, had given way to a focused intensity, a renewed sense of purpose that stemmed not from vengeance, but from a profound understanding of the fragility of life and the urgent necessity to protect it. The battle had unearthed a strength within her she hadn't known she possessed, a strength forged in the crucible of loss.

The sterile environment of the hospital, usually a symbol of healing and hope, felt stifling to Venga. She craved the familiar weight of her research, the comforting scent of aging books and parchment, the satisfying click of her laptop keys. The work, the intricate study of vampire lore and the city's hidden histories, had always been her sanctuary, her refuge from the brutal reality of the hunt. Now, it was more than a sanctuary; it was a shield, a weapon against the despair that threatened to engulf her.

Returning to her cluttered study, a space overflowing with ancient texts, forgotten maps, and technological equipment, was like returning home. The familiar chaos soothed her fractured soul. She found solace in the organization of her data, the relentless pursuit of knowledge, a path that seemed less like research and more like a pilgrimage.

The city's ley lines, previously just lines on a map, now held a profound significance. The fight with Samson had revealed their crucial role in the vampire's power, their convergence acting as a conduit, amplifying his strength, his very essence. Understanding this connection became her obsession, a quest not simply for knowledge, but for a way to protect the city, to prevent another tragedy like Chet's death from ever happening again.

Her research intensified, fueled by an unwavering determination. She spent countless hours poring over ancient texts, deciphering cryptic symbols, cross-referencing historical accounts with modern technological analysis. Her nights were filled with the glow of computer screens, the hum of servers, the quiet tap-tap-tap of her keyboard, the only sounds in her small apartment breaking the silence of her focused concentration.

She delved deeper into the city's hidden history, exploring forgotten catacombs, researching forgotten rituals, and unearthing long-buried secrets. She learned about forgotten wards, ancient protections that had once safeguarded the city from supernatural threats. These wards, long neglected, were now her focus.
Understanding their construction, their mechanics, and how to restore them became her new mission, her new fight.

The knowledge she acquired wasn't just academic; it was practical, tangible. It was the key to protecting the city, to preventing future attacks. Each discovered detail, each decoded symbol, each unearthed artifact filled her with a sense of purpose, a driving force that propelled her forward, defying the crippling grief that threatened to consume her.

She began to collaborate with experts from various fields—historians, geophysicists, even engineers— pooling her research findings and integrating their expertise into her ongoing study. The collaboration was challenging but invigorating, allowing her to expand her understanding and contribute to the collective effort. The shared goal united them and gave her a sense of camaraderie, a vital replacement for the bond she had lost with Chet.

Venga's renewed purpose wasn't solely about preventing future vampire attacks. It was about honoring Chet's memory, ensuring that his sacrifice was not in vain. She saw his death not as an ending, but as a catalyst, a call to action that transformed her grief into a powerful motivating force. She would not allow his death to be meaningless. His sacrifice would serve as a foundation for a stronger, more effective defense against the supernatural threats that lurked in the shadows of Salt Lake City.

The weight of her responsibility was immense, but Venga welcomed it. It was a weight she willingly bore, a burden she embraced. She was no longer just a hunter; she was a protector, a guardian of the city, a vigilant sentinel safeguarding its inhabitants from the unseen horrors that threatened to engulf it.

Days turned into weeks, and weeks into months. Venga's research progressed, and she started to see tangible results. She identified several locations where the ley lines were particularly potent, and she began to develop a plan to reinforce the city's defenses, utilizing her understanding of the ley lines and the ancient wards to create a protective barrier against supernatural threats.

Her transformation wasn't just intellectual; it was physical. She honed her skills, pushing her physical and mental limits, transforming her grief into raw, focused energy. She spent hours at the gym, building strength and stamina, preparing for whatever challenges lay ahead. The exhaustion was welcome; it was a physical manifestation of the effort she was putting into her work, a constant reminder of her commitment.

The physical changes were subtle yet significant. Her gaze was sharper, more intense; her movements, more precise, more decisive. The soft lines of her face had hardened, replaced by a steely determination that reflected her renewed purpose. She was stronger, both physically and mentally, tempered by loss and propelled by a burning desire to protect those she had sworn to defend.

One evening, as she sat reviewing her findings, the city lights painting the cityscape outside her window, a sense of quiet satisfaction washed over her. The grief was still there, a constant companion, but it no longer held the same power over her. It had been channeled, transformed into a driving force, an engine of her unwavering commitment. She had lost a comrade, but she had found a new purpose. The fight continued, but now it was fueled by more than just revenge or fear. It was fueled by a deep sense of responsibility, a commitment to protect the city, and a solemn promise to honor Chet's memory by ensuring his sacrifice wouldn't be in vain. The city would be safe, and she would be its shield. That was her renewed purpose, her new vow. The fight, far from being over, had just begun anew, strengthened by loss and fueled by a resolve forged in the fires of grief.

The rhythmic ticking of the grandfather clock in Venga's study was the only sound competing with the frantic tapping of her keyboard. Months had passed since the rooftop battle, months filled with the relentless pursuit of knowledge, the piecing together of a puzzle far more complex than she initially imagined. She'd mapped the city's ley lines with a precision bordering on obsession, charting their intricate pathways, their points of convergence, their subtle shifts and fluctuations. Her research had revealed a deeper, more unsettling truth about Samson Bordeau's connection to Salt Lake City –

a connection that went beyond simple exploitation of the city's energetic pathways. It was something… symbiotic.

The ancient texts she'd unearthed spoke of beings who weren't simply vampires, but entities who became intrinsically linked to the land, their essence woven into the very fabric of the city's energy grid. These weren't mere legends; the evidence was undeniable, etched in faded glyphs and cryptic symbols, confirmed by the geological data she'd painstakingly gathered. Samson wasn't just using the ley lines; he was becoming one with them, his essence bleeding into the city's energetic heart, leaving behind an imprint, a residue, a lingering shadow.

The chilling thought sent a shiver down her spine. Even with Samson's physical destruction, the threat hadn't vanished. It had simply transformed, becoming something far more insidious, far more difficult to eradicate. The city itself had been tainted, its energetic heartbeat echoing with the faint pulse of a vanquished predator. This wasn't just about preventing another vampire attack; this was about cleansing the city, about severing the connection Samson had forged, about exorcising the lingering shadow of his malevolent essence.

Her initial joy at successfully vanquishing Samson was now replaced by a gnawing unease, a deep-seated apprehension about the long-term consequences of their victory. The city felt different, quieter somehow, yet the silence was heavy, laden with an unspoken dread. The usual cacophony of urban life seemed muted, as if the city itself was holding its breath, waiting. Waiting for what? Venga didn't know, but the question hung in the air, a palpable tension that permeated everything.

She spent sleepless nights poring over historical accounts of similar events, searching for precedents, for clues to understanding the nature of Samson's lingering influence. She discovered tales of ancient entities, beings who had melded with the landscape, their presence subtly altering the very energy of the place, leaving a trail of unexplained phenomena in their wake. These weren't just stories; they were warnings. Warnings that she'd been too preoccupied with the immediate threat to fully comprehend.

The more she researched, the more disturbing the picture became. She found evidence of strange occurrences, unexplained phenomena that had become increasingly frequent since Samson's defeat. Reports of unsettling energy surges in unexpected locations, erratic fluctuations in the city's electromagnetic field, and unsettling reports from residents about strange occurrences they couldn't explain. Whispers of shadows moving on their own, of cold spots in otherwise warm homes, of a pervasive sense of unease that clung to the city like a shroud.

These weren't isolated incidents; they were patterns, a creeping tendril of something sinister, something that was growing, strengthening, feeding off the residual energy Samson had left behind. It was a disturbing manifestation of his lingering influence, a subtle but undeniable reminder of the battle that was still far from over. The victory was hollow, the sense of relief short-lived, replaced by a chilling awareness of a threat far more pervasive and far more difficult to confront.

Mike, despite his own physical and emotional scars, offered a grim yet stoic support. He understood the weight of Venga's findings, the terrifying implications of Samson's lingering presence. His silence was not one of despair but of grim determination. He'd seen firsthand the monster Samson had become, and he understood that even in death, the threat could evolve into something even more terrifying. He was ready, prepared to face whatever came next.

Ralph, still grappling with the trauma of Chet's death, found a renewed sense of purpose in helping Venga. His guilt, while still present, was now tempered by a grim determination to make amends, to prevent another tragedy. The loss of his friend had pushed him to the brink, but it had also ignited a fire within him, a desperate need to act, to contribute to the fight, however small his part might seem.

Their collaboration was born from shared grief and a shared determination. They accurately analyzed Venga's findings, integrating their respective skills to develop a plan to counteract Samson's lingering influence. They explored ancient rituals, technological solutions, and unconventional approaches, driven by a desperate need to protect the city, to prevent the subtle threat from blossoming into something catastrophic.

The task was daunting, the odds stacked against them. They were facing an enemy that wasn't a single entity, but a diffuse, insidious force, an energetic stain spread across the city's very foundations. The fight was no longer a direct confrontation; it was a battle against an intangible enemy, a relentless struggle against an ever-present threat.

As days bled into weeks, and weeks into months, the subtle changes in the city became more pronounced. The atmosphere grew heavier, the air colder. The feeling of unease was no longer a whisper; it was a scream barely suppressed, echoing through the city's silent streets. Strange occurrences were no longer isolated incidents, but a steady stream of unnerving events.

Venga, Mike, and Ralph worked tirelessly, pushing themselves to their limits. They faced setbacks, failures, and moments of despair, but their shared commitment, forged in the crucible of loss and fueled by a desperate hope, kept them moving forward. They knew they were in a race against time, a race against a spreading darkness that threatened to engulf the city. They were fighting not just for the city's survival, but for their own sanity, for the hope that the darkness could still be pushed back, that the shadow of Samson could be extinguished. The city, the shadows, the lingering essence of a vanquished vampire – it all hinted at a far greater, and far more terrifying battle to come. A battle that would test their limits, their courage, and their very souls. The fight was far from over. The shadow of Samson, though vanquished in physical form, still stretched long across Salt Lake City, and the hunters knew, with a chilling certainty, that the true reckoning was yet to come. The city waited, breath held, in the silent anticipation of the coming storm.

Chapter 5: The Legacy of the Hunt

The biting wind whipped around the small group gathered at the graveside, carrying with it the scent of damp earth and the faint, metallic tang of blood, a phantom echo of the rooftop battle. A scattering of mourners, mostly family and close friends of Chet, huddled together for warmth, their faces etched with grief. Venga, her usually vibrant eyes shadowed with exhaustion and sorrow, clutched a single, wilted crimson rose, its petals mirroring the blood that had stained the city's rooftops just months ago. Mike stood beside her, his broad shoulders slumped, a silent sentinel guarding her grief. Ralph, his usually boisterous spirit subdued, stared at the freshly turned earth, his gaze distant and haunted. The weight of their loss settled heavily upon them, a tangible presence that suffocated the air.

The service was simple, a stark contrast to the chaotic intensity of the hunts that had defined their lives. No grand pronouncements, no eulogies filled with hyperbolic praise. Just a quiet acknowledgment of a life cut short, a comrade lost. The priest, a kindly old man with eyes that held a depth of understanding born from years spent comforting the bereaved, spoke in hushed tones, his words a gentle balm to their raw wounds. He spoke of Chet's courage, his unwavering loyalty, his infectious laughter that had once filled their cramped headquarters with warmth. He spoke of the camaraderie they had shared, the bonds forged in the face of unspeakable horrors. He spoke of the emptiness they now felt, a void that would forever remain.

But his words, though comforting, failed to fully capture the essence of Chet. They couldn't encompass the man's quiet strength, his dry wit, his surprising talent for fixing anything mechanical, the way he always seemed to know when one of them needed a silent hand on their shoulder, a wordless understanding that transcended words. He was more than a hunter; he was family.

Ralph, breaking the somber silence, stepped forward. His voice, usually gravelly and filled with bravado, cracked with emotion as he spoke. He spoke of their shared training days, the grueling drills, the endless hours spent studying ancient texts, the uneasy camaraderie forged in the crucible of fear and adrenaline. He recounted their first real hunt, a terrifying encounter with a fledgling vampire in a forgotten alleyway, where Chet's quick thinking had saved them all. He remembered Chet's infectious grin as they celebrated small victories, the shared jokes and laughter that had become their anchor during the darkest moments. He spoke of Chet's unwavering belief in their cause, his unflinching commitment to protecting the innocent, even in the face of overwhelming odds. His voice choked, and tears streamed down his face, unashamed, unrestrained. The raw emotion resonated with those gathered around him, a shared grief that transcended words.

Venga, her composure momentarily breaking, approached him and placed a comforting hand on his arm. She hadn't spoken during the priest's words, but she felt Chet's absence keenly. His quiet strength, his unwavering loyalty, his gentle nature had been a constant support within their group, a stabilizing force during the chaos of their relentless hunts. His death had ripped a hole in their team, leaving behind a gaping void that threatened to consume them. He was their anchor, a quiet steadiness against the storms of their lives. Now that anchor was gone, leaving them adrift in a sea of sorrow.

Mike, ever stoic, spoke last. His words were few, but each one carried the weight of unspoken emotions. He spoke of Chet's unwavering courage in the face of unimaginable horrors, his resilience in the darkest of hours, his selfless dedication to their mission. He recalled the time Chet had saved his life during a particularly brutal encounter, shielding him from a deadly attack with his own body. He recounted moments not of grand heroism, but of quiet acts of kindness—a shared cup of coffee during a late night, a helping hand offered without words, a listening ear when they all needed someone to simply listen. These memories, not the adrenaline-fueled battles they fought, seemed to matter most.

The wind howled, a mournful symphony accompanying their silent farewells. As the final prayers were said and the last clods of earth were thrown onto the freshly dug grave, a profound sense of loss settled upon the group. It wasn't just the loss of a comrade; it was the loss of a part of themselves, a piece of their shared history, a bond severed that could never be truly mended.

Later, huddled in Venga's study, the familiar comfort of the flickering monitor light unable to dispel the lingering shadows of grief, they shared their remaining memories. They spoke of Chet's clumsy attempts at baking cookies that always seemed to burn, his encyclopedic knowledge of obscure horror films, his terrible puns that, somehow, always managed to elicit a chuckle. They spoke of his dreams – dreams that were now forever out of reach.

They found solace in their shared grief, in the recognition of their shared loss. The silence between them was no longer heavy with dread, but filled with the quiet weight of memory, a shared space of mourning where their tears mingled with the unspoken words of affection. The rhythmic ticking of the grandfather clock served as a grim reminder of the relentless march of time, a constant reminder that life moves on, even in the face of unbearable loss. But for those gathered in that small, dimly lit room, time seemed to stand still, suspended in a timeless moment of remembrance for their fallen comrade.

The memorial service, though brief and subdued, served as a necessary catharsis, a moment to acknowledge their grief, to honor their fallen friend, and to reaffirm the bonds that held them together. It was a painful process, a confrontation with their mortality and the fragility of life, but it was also a necessary step toward healing, a recognition of the loss that would forever shape their lives. The city outside, still tainted by Samson's lingering essence, held its breath. But inside Venga's study, the quiet, persistent ticking of the clock marked the passage of time, and for now, they found a fragile peace in their shared grief. The weight of the city's unspoken dread remained, a palpable presence, but in that small space, in the midst of their grief, there was a tentative beginning to the healing process. A healing that wouldn't erase their loss, but would allow them to carry Chet's memory, his strength, his quiet courage, forward into the continuing battle that lay ahead. A battle now even more desperate, made more poignant by the sacrifice of their friend. The fight continued, but now it was fought not only for the city, but for Chet, for the memory of their fallen comrade, for the legacy of their shared hunts. The shadow of Samson was gone, but the shadow of loss remained, a constant, aching reminder of the price of victory. And as the city waited, in silent apprehension, so too did the remaining hunters, preparing themselves for what the future might bring, knowing that the fight, though changed, was far from over. The memory of Chet, a beacon in their shared darkness, would guide them forward.

The weeks that followed Chet's funeral were a blur of quiet grief and determined action. The gaping hole in their team, the absence of his steady presence, was a constant ache, a phantom limb that throbbed with the memory of shared laughter and silent understanding. Yet, the city remained, a sprawling metropolis teetering on the precipice of chaos, still vulnerable to the unseen horrors that lurked in its shadows. They couldn't afford to succumb to their sorrow; the fight, though altered, continued. The legacy of the hunt, Chet's legacy, demanded it.

Mike, ever practical, took the lead in rebuilding their operations. His stoicism, usually a mask for deep emotions, was now tinged with a fierce determination. He knew Chet wouldn't want them to crumble; he would want them to be stronger, more vigilant, better prepared. He spearheaded the integration of new technology, driven by a desire to prevent future losses. They secured funding from a reluctant city council, fueled by a mixture of fear and grudging respect for the hunters' effectiveness. This wasn't just a fight against vampires anymore; it was a war against the unknown, a battle waged against the unseen forces that gnawed at the city's edges.

Venga, her grief simmering beneath a surface of controlled intensity, threw herself into research. She scoured ancient texts, cross-referencing them with modern scientific journals, searching for any clue, any insight that could give them an edge in the coming battles. She established a new network of informants, expanding their reach beyond the city's established boundaries. Her sharp mind, usually focused on tactical strategies, now sought deeper understanding of the ley lines, the mystical currents of energy that Samson had manipulated with such devastating effect. She believed understanding these currents was crucial to preventing future threats. The loss of Chet pushed her to delve deeper into the arcane, into the mysteries that lay at the heart of the supernatural world. She felt his loss acutely, but her grief fueled her relentless pursuit of knowledge, a quiet rebellion against the darkness that threatened to engulf them all.

Ralph, his boisterous spirit subdued but not extinguished, focused on upgrading their arsenal. The rooftop battle had highlighted their vulnerabilities; their weapons, though effective, needed improvement. He spent countless hours in his workshop, a chaotic symphony of clanking metal and sizzling sparks, tinkering, modifying, creating. He designed new crossbow bolts tipped with silver infused with a potent concoction of Venga's creation, a potent formula designed to neutralize the fog-vampires' ethereal abilities. He developed advanced UV-emitting devices, far more potent and portable than their previous equipment, allowing them to strike faster and more effectively. His usual gruff exterior hid a growing determination; he wouldn't let Chet's death be in vain. Every modification, every upgrade, was a testament to their fallen comrade, a silent vow to continue the fight.

He channeled his grief into action, forging new weapons, new strategies, a new commitment to the cause that now felt more personal, more profound than ever before.

The rebuilding wasn't just about technology and tactics; it was about rebuilding their team. The loss of Chet had created a void, a space of silence that echoed with his absence. Filling that void required not just new equipment, but new trust, new shared understanding. They brought in a new recruit, Maya, a young woman with a sharp mind and an even sharper wit. She was an expert in digital forensics, capable of sifting through data and uncovering hidden connections that others might miss. Maya, despite her initial apprehension about joining a team still mourning a loss, brought a fresh perspective and a much-needed infusion of hope. She impressed them with her quick thinking, her dedication, and her surprisingly practical approach to vampire hunting. Mike, Ralph, and Venga recognized her potential and worked to integrate her seamlessly into their already tight-knit group.

The addition of Maya was a symbol of their resilience, their commitment to carrying on, despite their loss. They embraced the changes, the new technologies, the new strategies, as steps toward securing a safer future. Their headquarters, once a cramped, dimly lit apartment, was transformed into a state-of-the-art operational center. The walls were lined with monitors displaying real-time data streams, maps of the city's ley lines, and detailed profiles of potential threats. The air hummed with the quiet thrum of advanced technology, a stark contrast to the grimy atmosphere of their earlier hunts. They used the latest in thermal imaging, sound detection and even subtle psychic sensors that Venga's research had unearthed, providing early warnings of unseen threats.

Their training regimens intensified. They pushed themselves harder, both physically and mentally, striving for peak performance. They knew that the next encounter might not be as forgiving as the previous ones. They spent long hours refining their combat techniques, perfecting their coordination, and improving their individual skills. They learned to compensate for Chet's absence, adapting their strategies, distributing his responsibilities, filling the gaps he'd left behind. The transition wasn't easy; the memories of Chet's quiet strength and unwavering loyalty were constant reminders of what they'd lost. But they pressed on, driven by a shared sense of purpose, a commitment to honor his sacrifice. The fight wasn't personal only in the sense that they were fighting for the city; it was also intensely personal because they were fighting for Chet's memory, for his legacy. Their shared grief, though profound, became the fuel that propelled them forward, pushing them to achieve a level of preparedness they hadn't thought possible.

The city, however, remained an uneasy place. The shadow of Samson, though gone, cast a long pall over the city. The lingering unease, the constant apprehension, was a palpable presence, a silent testament to the fragility of their safety. But they pressed on, their grief tempered by a burgeoning determination. They were rebuilding, not only their lives and their team, but their faith in themselves, their faith in their ability to protect the city, their faith in the legacy of the hunt. They carried Chet's memory not as a burden, but as a beacon, guiding them through the darkness, reminding them of the courage, the loyalty, and the quiet strength that had defined their fallen comrade, and pushing them to forge a future worthy of his sacrifice. The fight continued, but now it was stronger, more resolute, and powered by the enduring spirit of the fallen comrade who had shown them what true courage truly meant. The legacy of the hunt was secure; it would continue, stronger than ever, bearing the mark of its losses, its wounds, its unwavering determination.

The weight of Chet's absence settled heavily on Mike's shoulders, a physical pressure that mirrored the emotional burden he carried. He wasn't just the team leader anymore; he was the anchor, the steady hand guiding them through the turbulent waters of grief and the relentless pursuit of the unseen. His stoicism, once a shield, now felt like a cage, constricting his emotions but fueling his determination. He understood the necessity of moving forward, of honoring Chet's memory not through sorrow but through action.

His new role wasn't just about leading hunts; it was about forging a new generation of hunters, imbued with the same dedication and skill that Chet had embodied. He initiated a rigorous training program, pushing the recruits to their limits, both physically and mentally. The old methods were insufficient; they needed to evolve, to adapt to the changing landscape of the supernatural world. Mike designed a curriculum that incorporated advanced combat techniques, incorporating elements of both modern martial arts and ancient hunting rituals. He methodically planned drills, simulating real-world scenarios—ambushes in darkened alleyways, rooftop confrontations, close-quarters battles in cramped, claustrophobic spaces.

The training ground was a former warehouse on the city's outskirts, a sprawling, echoing space where the ghosts of past battles seemed to linger. Here, under Mike's watchful eye, the recruits learned to move silently, to anticipate their enemy's attacks, to react instinctively. He emphasized the importance of teamwork, the seamless coordination that had been their strength in previous hunts, the silent understanding that allowed them to anticipate each other's moves. He stressed the need for adaptability, for the ability to improvise and overcome unexpected obstacles, characteristics that Chet had possessed in abundance. He drove them relentlessly, pushing them beyond their perceived limits, shaping them into hunters worthy of the legacy they were inheriting.

Maya, the newest addition to the team, was a testament to Mike's evolving leadership style. She was initially hesitant, her youth and inexperience contrasting sharply with the grim determination of the seasoned hunters. Mike didn't pressure her; he recognized her potential, her sharp mind, her ability to analyze data and identify patterns that others missed. He focused on nurturing her skills, providing her with tailored training that honed her strengths while addressing her weaknesses. He patiently guided her through the complexities of vampire hunting, explaining the nuances of ancient lore alongside the latest technological advancements. He introduced her to Venga's research, explaining the city's ley lines and the supernatural currents that flowed beneath their feet.

Their training wasn't solely confined to combat. Mike instilled in them the importance of understanding the enemy, of studying their patterns, their weaknesses, their vulnerabilities. He taught them the history of fog-vampires, sharing stories passed down through generations of hunters, cautionary tales of past encounters, the desperate battles fought in the shadowed corners of the city. He showed them the tools of the trade, explaining the intricacies of each weapon, the subtle differences in their effectiveness, the importance of precision and timing. He spent hours discussing the moral complexities of their work, emphasizing the thin line between hunter and hunted, the ethical considerations that guided their actions.

One particularly grueling exercise involved navigating a labyrinthine network of tunnels beneath the city, a claustrophobic maze that tested their endurance, their courage, and their ability to work as a team. The air was thick with the smell of damp earth and decay, the darkness pressing in on all sides. Mike led the way, his movements fluid and precise, his senses honed to a razor's edge. He guided Maya through the treacherous passages, teaching her to rely on her instincts, to trust her senses, to anticipate danger before it struck. He explained the subtle shifts in temperature, the faintest whispers of movement, the almost imperceptible changes in air pressure that signaled the presence of unseen entities.

Another training session focused on using the advanced technology they had acquired. He showed them the thermal imaging equipment, teaching them to distinguish between human and supernatural heat signatures, to identify potential threats hidden in the shadows. He demonstrated the UV-emitting devices, explaining how they could be used to disorient and neutralize fog-vampires, temporarily blinding them, disrupting their ethereal abilities. He painstakingly detailed the intricacies of the psychic sensors, explaining how they could detect the subtle disturbances in the psychic field caused by supernatural beings, providing early warnings of impending attacks. He showed them the importance of cross-referencing the technological data with Venga's mystical insights, emphasizing the need for a holistic approach to vampire hunting, a balance between the modern and the ancient.

Mike's instruction extended beyond the purely tactical. He recognized the importance of mental fortitude, the ability to control fear and maintain focus under pressure. He introduced meditation techniques, teaching them to clear their minds, to calm their nerves, to access a deeper level of awareness. He emphasized the importance of teamwork, the bond of trust and shared understanding that bound the hunters together. He encouraged them to share their fears, their anxieties, their doubts, recognizing that vulnerability was not a sign of weakness but a strength, a testament to their humanity.

His leadership style was a blend of his former stoicism and a newly acquired compassion, a reflection of Chet's influence. He wasn't just ordering them around; he was mentoring them, nurturing their potential, guiding them through the emotional and physical challenges of their dangerous profession. He shared his own experiences, his past failures and triumphs, illustrating the lessons he had learned, the pitfalls he had encountered, the strategies he had developed. He listened to their concerns, answered their questions, and offered support without judgement. He fostered an environment of trust and mutual respect, a crucial element in their fight against the unseen horrors that plagued their city.

He showed them how to interpret the subtle signs of supernatural activity, how to decipher the cryptic messages left by the vampires, how to analyze the patterns of their attacks. He taught them the importance of patience, the need for detailed observation, the subtle art of deduction. He instilled in them the unwavering conviction that their fight was not only a battle against evil but a fight for the preservation of humanity itself.

Mike's transformation wasn't solely about adapting to the changes within their team. It was about understanding the larger picture, the deep-seated forces that drove the supernatural occurrences in Salt Lake City. He began studying the city's history more deeply, delving into its forgotten lore and the hidden currents of energy that flowed beneath its streets. He recognized that the fight against Samson Bordeau had merely scratched the surface of a far larger, more insidious threat.

The training continued, but it now had a different focus. It wasn't just about killing vampires; it was about understanding them, about understanding the forces that created them, the mystical currents that fueled their existence. Mike's new role was a reflection of this shift, a testament to his evolving perspective, a legacy forged in the crucible of loss and tempered by the enduring flame of his determination. He was not only preparing his team for future hunts; he was preparing them for a war. A war against the unknown, a war fought not only on the rooftops and in the shadowed alleys, but in the minds and hearts of those who fought for the soul of the city. The legacy of the hunt now rested not just on the shoulders of Mike alone, but on the shoulders of a new generation, ready to face the darkness, carrying with them the memory of Chet, and the unwavering resolve forged in the fires of their shared grief.

Ralph, ever the pragmatist, saw the loss of Chet not as an end, but as a catalyst for change. He'd always been the brains of the operation, the quiet inventor whose gadgets and gizmos often proved the difference between life and death. Now, fueled by a grim determination to prevent future losses, he poured all his energy into refining their arsenal and developing new technologies to combat the city's growing supernatural threat. His workshop, a chaotic jumble of wires, circuit boards, and arcane artifacts, became his sanctuary, a place where the ghosts of past battles were replaced by the hum of innovation.

His first project was an upgrade to their UV emitters. The older models, while effective, had a limited range and were cumbersome to use. Ralph designed a new generation of devices, smaller, more powerful, and integrated with a targeting system that used thermal imaging to pinpoint fog-vampires with pinpoint accuracy. These weren't simply blinding lights anymore; they were precision weapons, capable of delivering focused bursts of UV radiation that could temporarily incapacitate even the strongest vampires, buying precious seconds in a life-or-death struggle. He also incorporated a silent operational mode, allowing them to use the devices without alerting the vampires to their presence. The prototypes were tested rigorously in the abandoned warehouse, the blinding flashes illuminating the dusty corners as Mike's team practiced their newly refined combat techniques.

Next, Ralph turned his attention to the psychic sensors. Venga's insights into the city's ley lines had proven invaluable, but translating those insights into tangible, usable data had been a challenge. Ralph designed a sophisticated algorithm that correlated Venga's readings with the sensor data, creating a predictive model that could anticipate vampire movements with surprising accuracy. The system could not only detect the presence of supernatural entities, but it could also predict their likely paths, their points of vulnerability, and even anticipate their attack patterns. This wasn't simply about reacting to threats; it was about preempting them, gaining the upper hand before the fight even began. He visualized the data as a three-dimensional map displayed on a heads-up display, allowing the team to see the "flow" of supernatural energy and the location of potential threats in real-time. The system even incorporated a proximity alarm that would alert the team of nearby paranormal activity.

But Ralph's innovations went beyond simple upgrades. He began experimenting with new weapons altogether, drawing inspiration from both ancient lore and cutting-edge technology. His research into alchemical formulas, gleaned from Venga's collection of grimoires and obscure texts, led him to develop a potent concoction that could neutralize a fog-vampire's ability to manipulate the fog, essentially grounding them and rendering them vulnerable to conventional weapons. The process was complex, requiring precision and careful timing, but the results were astonishingly effective. The concoction, delivered via a specially designed dart gun, temporarily disrupted the vampire's ethereal connection to the city's ley lines, leaving them disoriented and weakened.

He also developed a new type of stake, crafted from a rare, vibrantly blue metal he'd discovered in an abandoned mine shaft. This metal, possessing unique properties that he'd only begun to understand, appeared to have a natural affinity for repelling supernatural energies. The stakes, thoroughly forged and sharpened, were not just weapons; they were conduits, capable of focusing and amplifying the hunter's energy, making them far more effective against even the most powerful vampires. He designed the stakes with specialized grips, ensuring that they would not slip during a struggle.

His most ambitious project, however, was a device he called the "Ley Line Disruptor." Based on Venga's research, Ralph theorized that by manipulating the city's ley lines, they could disrupt the fog-vampires' power source, effectively weakening them en masse. This was a high-risk, high-reward endeavor, potentially capable of crippling the entire vampire population but also potentially causing unforeseen consequences. The Disruptor was a complex device, a fusion of technology and ancient magic, requiring precise calibration and a deep understanding of the city's underlying mystical currents. Its design resembled a large, intricately carved orb, pulsing with internal energy, capable of generating a focused beam of anti-magical energy.

The creation of the Ley Line Disruptor was a collaborative effort, requiring Ralph's technological expertise and Venga's mystical knowledge. They spent weeks in Ralph's workshop, poring over ancient texts, conducting experiments, and testing prototypes. Venga, initially skeptical of Ralph's approach, became increasingly impressed by his ingenuity, her mystical insights proving crucial in guiding Ralph's technological development. They argued, debated, and refined their ideas, their collaboration a testament to the power of combining ancient wisdom with modern science. The process was slow, painstaking, and sometimes fraught with near-misses, but their shared determination pushed them forward.

The testing phase was even more challenging. The Ley Line Disruptor was powerful, potentially dangerous, capable of disrupting not just the vampires but potentially the city's delicate balance of supernatural energies. They conducted their tests in remote areas on the outskirts of Salt Lake City, carefully monitoring the effects of the device on the surrounding environment. They found that a precise calibration of the device was crucial. Too much energy and they risked causing unpredictable surges of mystical energy, possibly creating new, more dangerous entities; too little energy and it was ineffective.

Ralph, always scrupulous, documented every detail, every success, and every failure. He even created elaborate simulations to model the potential effects of the Disruptor on the vampire population. These simulations, incorporating data from past encounters and their improved psychic sensors, allowed them to predict the possible outcomes of using the device in different locations and under varying conditions. This diligence, his relentless pursuit of perfection, ensured that when they finally used the Disruptor in the final confrontation, it would be with a calculated precision, minimizing risks and maximizing its effectiveness.

But Ralph's contributions extended beyond the tangible. He'd also developed sophisticated data analysis tools, allowing the team to quickly process information gathered during hunts and identify patterns in the vampires' behavior. This allowed for a more proactive, intelligence-driven approach to hunting, helping to anticipate attacks and predict vampire movements with remarkable accuracy. The data analysis also revealed subtle connections between the fog-vampires and the city's ley lines, insights that were essential in developing the Ley Line Disruptor and understanding the true extent of the supernatural threat.

Ralph's innovations were not simply technological advancements; they were a testament to his unwavering commitment to his team and his city. He'd lost Chet, and he refused to let that loss be in vain. His inventions, born from grief and fueled by determination, represented the evolution of vampire hunting, the fusion of ancient wisdom and modern technology, a powerful force in the ongoing battle against the shadows that haunted Salt Lake City. His legacy, alongside Chet's, would be one of innovation and sacrifice, a testament to the enduring human spirit in the face of overwhelming darkness. The silent hum of his inventions, echoing in the quiet corners of his workshop, was a promise – a promise that the fight would continue, that the darkness would not win, and that the city would be safe, at least for now.

Venga, her face pale but determined, stared at the swirling patterns etched into the ancient grimoire. The flickering candlelight cast long, dancing shadows across her cluttered study, illuminating shelves overflowing with books, artifacts, and strange, unsettling objects collected over years of research. The death of Chet had shaken her profoundly, but it had also ignited a fire within her, a fierce resolve to understand the forces they were fighting, to gain an advantage over the creatures of the night that preyed on Salt Lake City. Ralph's technological advancements were impressive, but Venga knew that true victory lay in understanding the underlying supernatural forces at play.

She traced a finger along the faded script, deciphering the cryptic symbols that spoke of ancient rituals and forgotten powers. This particular grimoire, a rare find from a forgotten monastery in the Himalayas, detailed the intricate network of ley lines that pulsed beneath Salt Lake City, acting as conduits for magical energy. It described not just their location, but also their fluctuating strengths and the ways in which they influenced the supernatural landscape. She had already shared her initial findings with Ralph, contributing significantly to the development of his Ley Line Disruptor. But this grimoire held secrets far deeper, hinting at a complexity far beyond what she had initially imagined.

The grimoire spoke of nodes, points of intense magical energy where the ley lines converged, creating potent vortexes of power. These nodes, she learned, weren't merely geographical locations; they were also points of vulnerability, places where the veil between worlds thinned, allowing supernatural entities to manifest more easily. Samson Bordeau, the fog-vampire they had recently vanquished, had clearly drawn strength from one such node, his power amplified by the concentrated magical energy. Understanding these nodes, Venga realized, was crucial to preventing future attacks. She needed to locate every node in the city, map their strengths, and understand how they interacted with each other.

Her research extended far beyond the grimoire. She delved into forgotten archives, scouring city records, historical documents, and obscure occult texts for any mention of ley lines or supernatural activity in Salt Lake City. She discovered anecdotal accounts dating back centuries, whispers of strange occurrences, unexplained phenomena, and unsettling legends passed down through generations. These fragmented narratives, often dismissed as folklore or superstition, now held a new significance, each piece of the puzzle contributing to a larger, more terrifying picture.

She spent hours poring over old maps, overlaying them with her own readings from the psychic sensors Ralph had developed. She methodically charted the locations of reported supernatural incidents, comparing them to the ley line network mapped out in the grimoire. The correlation was striking. Many incidents, ranging from unexplained disappearances to bizarre accidents, clustered around the nodes of intense magical energy, suggesting a clear connection between the ley lines and the city's supernatural activity.

Venga's research wasn't limited to the ley lines. She discovered references to other supernatural entities, beings far older and more powerful than the fog-vampires. One particularly disturbing passage described the existence of "Nightgaunts," creatures of pure shadow, said to feed on fear and despair. These entities, the grimoire claimed, were bound to the city, their power tied to the city's collective anxieties and darkest secrets. The more fear the city harbored, the stronger they became.

This realization sent a shiver down Venga's spine. It explained the seemingly random nature of some of the attacks. The fog-vampires weren't simply acting on their own; they were being influenced, perhaps even controlled, by these shadowy entities. It added a chilling layer to the fight they were engaged in. It was no longer simply about hunting down individual vampires; it was about confronting a far larger, more insidious threat.

She found further evidence of this larger threat in her investigation into the city's history. She discovered that Salt Lake City was built on sacred ground, a place of immense mystical significance to various indigenous tribes. These tribes, long before the arrival of European settlers, had practiced rituals and ceremonies to harness the power of the ley lines, maintaining a fragile balance between the human world and the supernatural realm. The city's modern development, she realized, had disrupted this balance, unleashing forces that had long been dormant.

This understanding was crucial. It gave her a new perspective on the fog-vampires, not just as mindless predators but as pawns in a larger, more sinister game. The disruption of the ley lines, caused by the city's expansion, had created an imbalance, providing an opportunity for these entities to gain power and influence. This also explained why the fog-vampires seemed to be growing stronger, more aggressive, and more numerous.

The deeper Venga dug, the more disturbing the truth became. She found evidence suggesting a connection between the ley lines and the city's infrastructure, the power grid, the water supply, even the very fabric of the city itself. The supernatural and the mundane were intertwined, inextricably linked. A disruption in one realm could trigger a cascade of unforeseen consequences in the other.

This realization underscored the importance of Ralph's Ley Line Disruptor. But it also highlighted the inherent risks. Manipulating the ley lines, even with the precision Ralph was striving for, was a dangerous gamble. They were playing with forces they didn't fully understand, potentially unleashing even greater chaos. Venga's research wasn't just about understanding the enemy; it was about understanding the delicate balance of the city's supernatural ecosystem and the catastrophic consequences of disrupting it.

Her research intensified. Night after night, she poured over ancient texts, consulted obscure maps, and analyzed data from the psychic sensors, seeking a deeper understanding of the city's supernatural architecture. She tirelessly pieced together the fragments of knowledge, weaving them into a tapestry of arcane lore and scientific data, a complex network that revealed the terrifying truth about Salt Lake City's haunted history and the ongoing battle for its soul. Her work was far from over; in fact, it had just begun. The stakes were higher than ever, the threat far greater than any of them had initially imagined. The legacy of the hunt wasn't simply about defeating the fog-vampires; it was about understanding, and perhaps even controlling, the forces that shaped the very reality of their city. And Venga, driven by grief and a relentless pursuit of knowledge, was determined to uncover all the secrets, no matter the cost. The city's survival, she knew, depended on it.

Chapter 6: Whispers in the City

The silence that followed the demise of Samson Bordeau was not the peaceful quiet of victory. It was a tense, expectant silence, heavy with the unspoken knowledge that the battle was far from over. Salt Lake City, cleansed of the immediate fog-vampire threat, seemed to hold its breath, waiting. The city's usual cacophony – the rumble of traffic, the chatter of crowds, the distant sirens – felt muted, replaced by an unnerving stillness that prickled the skin.

This sense of unease began subtly. A lingering chill in the air, even on the warmest days, a feeling of being watched, even in broad daylight. The shadows seemed deeper, longer, and more menacing, as if something lurked just beyond the periphery of vision. Then came the whispers.

Not literal whispers, not the rustling of leaves or the murmur of voices, but a pervasive sense of unseen communication, a subtle shift in the city's energy, an unsettling hum beneath the surface of everyday life. People started reporting strange occurrences – fleeting glimpses of figures in the periphery, shadows that moved independently of their source, objects misplaced, then reappearing in odd locations. The city's collective unease grew into a palpable thing, a heavy blanket suffocating the vibrancy that had briefly returned.

Mike, still reeling from the loss of Chet, found himself increasingly irritable, his senses hyper-alert, picking up on subtle shifts in the air that others dismissed as mere coincidence. He found himself constantly scanning the shadows, his hand instinctively reaching for the familiar weight of his weapon. Sleep offered little respite; his nights were filled with restless dreams of swirling fog and the chilling rasp of unseen things.

Ralph, despite his technological advancements and the satisfaction of his successful Ley Line Disruptor, felt the same unsettling shift. His sensors, usually so reliable, sputtered and flickered, delivering erratic readings, registering bursts of inexplicable energy that defied explanation. The city's ley lines, which he had mapped with such detailed precision, seemed to be behaving erratically, pulsing with an unusual intensity. Their previously predictable patterns were now chaotic, a discordant symphony of energy.

Even Venga, despite her deep knowledge of the city's supernatural undercurrents, felt the growing unease. Her research, which had initially provided a sense of understanding and control, now felt inadequate, leaving her with a growing sense of vulnerability. The ancient grimoire, her constant companion, offered no immediate answers to this new threat; its cryptic verses seemed to hint at something far more ancient, far more insidious, than the fog-vampires.

The increased police reports initially dismissed as pranks and mistaken identity were becoming too numerous to ignore. Unexplained disappearances in the quieter, more secluded areas of Salt Lake City, particularly around the nodes Venga had identified, were reported with increasing frequency. Witnesses spoke of chilling encounters, unsettling sights, and a lingering sense of dread that clung to them long after the incidents themselves.

One particularly unsettling incident involved a group of teenagers exploring an abandoned warehouse near the city's oldest cemetery, a place Venga knew to be situated directly above a significant ley line node. The teenagers, initially excited by the thrill of urban exploration, emerged hours later, pale and trembling, recounting a story of a dark, oppressive presence that seemed to feed on their fear. They described fleeting glimpses of shadowy figures, their eyes burning with an unearthly light. The lingering sense of dread and fear emanating from them affected the officers investigating, and even seasoned detectives felt a palpable chill.

Another report came from a lone hiker on the foothills surrounding the city. He recounted an encounter with an unnatural fog, denser than any he had ever witnessed, which seemed to engulf him, leaving him with a profound sense of disorientation and an unsettling emptiness. He claimed to have seen figures within the fog, impossibly tall and slender, their forms dissolving and reforming like smoke. His words were disjointed and confused, yet the primal fear in his eyes was undeniable.

Ralph's sensors, when pointed towards the areas where these incidents occurred, recorded unusual spikes in electromagnetic activity, accompanied by erratic fluctuations in temperature and atmospheric pressure. These readings, though perplexing, confirmed that something unnatural was at play, something far beyond the capabilities of ordinary scientific explanation.

Venga realized, with a growing sense of dread, that they were dealing with a new threat, a threat that operated on a different plane of existence, a threat that exploited the city's fears and anxieties. The fog-vampires had been merely a symptom, a manifestation of something far greater, something lurking in the shadows, waiting for its moment.

The unsettling atmosphere wasn't confined to isolated incidents. It permeated the entire city. A pervasive sense of dread replaced the fleeting joy of the city's newfound peace, replacing the lightheartedness with a creeping unease that was beginning to spread like a contagion. The previously vibrant streets felt eerily empty, even during peak hours. The usual laughter and chatter were replaced by a nervous silence, a collective holding of breath.

The city's collective subconscious, the repository of its hopes, dreams, and fears, seemed to be manifesting itself in a terrifyingly tangible way. This wasn't a simple case of isolated supernatural occurrences; it was an awakening, a rising of something ancient and sinister, fueled by the city's own hidden anxieties. The darker aspects of Salt Lake City, long dormant, were emerging, clawing their way into reality.

Mike, Ralph, and Venga found themselves facing a new and far more formidable enemy. An enemy that wasn't a singular entity, but a collective, a force that existed in the shadows, feeding on the very essence of the city's fears and vulnerabilities. The battle against Samson Bordeau had been brutal, but it was only the prelude to a far more terrifying conflict. The whispers in the city were growing louder, more insistent, and the uneasy silence was about to be shattered. The feeling of impending doom hung heavy in the air, a tangible presence that chilled them to the bone, whispering promises of a nightmare far beyond anything they had yet encountered. Their fight for Salt Lake City had just begun anew. The city, once again, held its breath, waiting for the darkness to descend.

The unease wasn't confined to whispered rumors and unsettling encounters. It seeped into the very fabric of Salt Lake City, transforming the familiar into something alien and terrifying. The city's vibrant energy, the boisterous spirit that had briefly returned after Samson's defeat, was replaced by a chilling stillness, a pervasive sense of dread that hung heavy in the air like a shroud.

The normally bustling streets felt deserted, even during peak hours. Shops that had once overflowed with customers now stood eerily empty, their windows reflecting the city's palpable fear. The laughter and chatter that once filled the air were replaced by a nervous silence, broken only by the occasional, hurried footsteps of passersby, their eyes darting nervously at the shadows. Even the ubiquitous Mormon Tabernacle Choir, usually a beacon of peace and harmony, seemed to carry a note of melancholic foreboding in its hymns.

The changes were subtle at first, almost imperceptible. Streetlights flickered erratically, casting long, dancing shadows that seemed to have a life of their own.

Doors creaked open and shut without explanation, and objects vanished only to reappear in unexpected places. The city's infrastructure, usually so robust and reliable, began to malfunction – traffic lights went haywire, power surges disrupted communication networks, and even the intricate water system seemed to behave erratically.

These were not mere technical glitches; they were symptoms, manifestations of a deeper, more sinister force at work. It was as if the city itself was groaning under an unseen weight, struggling to contain something ancient and malevolent that was stirring within its depths.

Ralph, despite his technological prowess, felt increasingly helpless. His sophisticated sensors, designed to detect even the slightest anomalies, were overwhelmed by the chaotic energy that permeated the city. The ley lines, which he had painstakingly mapped, were now a chaotic mess, pulsing with an unpredictable intensity that defied his understanding. The data he collected was a meaningless jumble of erratic spikes and inexplicable fluctuations, offering no clue as to the source of the disturbance.

Venga, her usual calm demeanor replaced by a growing sense of unease, delved deeper into her research. The ancient grimoire, her guide through the city's supernatural undercurrents, revealed cryptic clues about a forgotten entity, a primordial being tied to the very foundation of Salt Lake City. The grimoire spoke of a slumbering entity, a creature of immense power that fed on fear and despair, its awakening heralded by a confluence of specific astrological alignments and supernatural events.

Mike, haunted by Chet's death and burdened by the weight of responsibility, found himself increasingly isolated. His hyper-vigilance, honed by years of battling supernatural threats, turned into paranoia. He saw enemies in every shadow, every fleeting movement in his peripheral vision. His nights were plagued by vivid nightmares, where he was relentlessly pursued by unseen horrors through a labyrinth of twisting streets and shadowy alleys. The city's fear became his own, amplifying his existing trauma and driving him to the brink of madness.

The police department was overwhelmed. Reports poured in from every corner of the city – strange sounds in the night, unexplained disappearances, unsettling encounters with shadowy figures, objects moving on their own accord. Witnesses described a growing sense of dread, a chilling feeling of being watched, even in broad daylight. The police, initially skeptical, found themselves increasingly unnerved by the sheer volume and consistency of these reports. Even seasoned officers, hardened by years of facing crime and violence, found themselves struggling to maintain their composure.

The incidents were not random occurrences. They seemed to cluster around specific locations – the old cemetery, the abandoned warehouse near the Jordan River, a series of forgotten tunnels beneath the city. Venga realized that these locations corresponded to significant ley line nodes, points of concentrated supernatural energy that had been disturbed, creating rifts in the fabric of reality. It was through these rifts that the new threat was manifesting itself, seeping into the city like a creeping poison.

One particularly horrifying incident involved a young family living in a seemingly ordinary suburban house. The father, a well-respected lawyer, awoke one night to find his wife and child gone, their beds empty, no sign of forced entry. Only a lingering scent of ozone and a faint, chilling whisper, barely audible above the hum of the refrigerator, remained. Similar disappearances, all connected to the ley lines, followed, leaving behind a growing trail of inexplicable vanishing acts.

As the city teetered on the brink of chaos, Mike, Ralph, and Venga knew they faced a challenge unlike any they had ever encountered. The fog-vampires had been a singular threat, a problem that could be solved with enough force and determination. But the new entity they faced was a force of nature, a malevolent presence that fed on the city's deepest fears and anxieties, manipulating the very fabric of reality to its own ends.

Their fight was not just for the survival of Salt Lake City, but for the preservation of its soul. The whispers in the city were growing louder, the shadows deeper, and the chilling sense of dread more pervasive. The battle for Salt Lake City was far from over. It was, in fact, only just beginning, a battle against a force that threatened not only the city's physical safety but also the fragile sanity of its inhabitants. The darkness that had once threatened to consume the city from the outside now threatened to emerge from within, to manifest from the city's collective fear and uncertainty. The hunters, once victorious, now found themselves facing a foe that mirrored the deepest anxieties of the human heart.

The chilling silence of Salt Lake City pressed down on Mike like a physical weight. The city's collective fear, a palpable entity, clung to him, amplifying the already gnawing anxiety that had taken root after Chet's death. He couldn't shake the image of his fallen comrade, the life draining from his eyes, the desperate, silent scream frozen on his face. That image, a stark reminder of their vulnerability, fueled Mike's relentless pursuit of answers. He couldn't afford to let another friend become a victim. He couldn't afford to fail the city.

He eschewed the team's coordinated efforts for now, needing the solitude to process the chaotic jumble of information that had emerged since Samson's demise. The official police reports were a frustratingly vague collection of eyewitness accounts, ranging from the bizarre to the terrifying. Unexplained disappearances, whispers in the dead of night, objects moving on their own – the patterns were elusive, the connections unclear. Ralph's technological prowess was proving useless against this new foe, his advanced sensors overwhelmed by the unpredictable surges of chaotic energy emanating from the city's ley lines. Venga, with her ancient texts and arcane knowledge, offered cryptic clues but no clear solution. Mike knew he had to find a different path, a more direct route to the heart of this new horror.

He began his investigation in the city's oldest district, a labyrinth of crumbling brick buildings and forgotten alleys, steeped in a history as dark and complex as the city's present predicament. He started with the reports of unexplained disappearances, thoroughly tracing the routes of the victims, searching for a common thread, a pattern that could illuminate the nature of the threat. He spent days poring over maps, satellite images, and old city records, searching for any detail that could offer a clue.

His first breakthrough came in the form of a faded photograph unearthed from the city archives – a picture of a construction project from the early 1900s. The image showed a group of workers standing around a deep excavation, their faces etched with a strange mixture of awe and fear. In the background, hidden amongst the scaffolding and construction equipment, Mike noticed something unusual – a swirling vortex of energy, barely visible, captured only at the edge of the photograph. This was more than a photographic anomaly; it was a suggestion of the city's supernatural underbelly. He zoomed in, his heart pounding as a faint, shimmering energy flickered at the edges of the poorly resolved image.

Further investigation revealed that the excavation had been hastily abandoned, shrouded in secrecy. Official reports spoke of "unforeseen geological challenges," but Mike sensed a darker truth. He followed the trail, piecing together the fragments of forgotten history, until he uncovered a local legend, a whispered tale of a forgotten entity, a slumbering beast buried deep beneath the city's foundations. This creature, the stories suggested, was bound to the city's ley lines, its power amplified by the city's fear and despair. The abandoned excavation site, Mike realized, was directly above one of the most potent ley line nodes.

Armed with this information, Mike returned to the site, now a deserted patch of overgrown land, a testament to the city's forgotten past. He searched the area methodically, his senses heightened, his every nerve on edge. He uncovered fragments of strange, obsidian-like shards, scattered amongst the weeds and rubble. These shards resonated with a faint, pulsating energy, an energy that felt both ancient and terrifyingly alive. The obsidian shards seemed to whisper secrets, their smooth, cold surfaces sending shivers down his spine.

The whispers weren't audible, but they resonated deep within him, disturbing images flashing through his mind – shadows dancing in the corners of his vision, distorted faces peering from the darkness, chilling echoes of laughter and despair. He knew then that these were not just fragments of some forgotten construction project; these were artifacts, remnants of a far more ancient and sinister history. The fragments were resonating with the same chaotic energy he'd detected emanating from the ley lines, a connection that cemented his suspicion.

As darkness fell, the whispers intensified, weaving themselves into the city's growing unease. The city itself seemed to be groaning under the weight of the dormant entity, its fear amplifying the creature's power. Mike felt the city's dread as his own, the weight of its collective fear pressing down on him, threatening to overwhelm him. The feeling was suffocating, a chilling premonition of what was to come. He knew, with bone-deep certainty, that this wasn't just about stopping the entity. It was about confronting the darkness that lurked within the hearts of men, the fear that gave the entity its power.

Mike's investigation led him to the city library, where he spent countless nights poring over historical records and obscure texts. He uncovered newspaper clippings detailing strange occurrences from the city's past, accounts of unexplained disappearances and bizarre accidents, all clustering around locations corresponding to the ley line nodes. The patterns were subtle, almost imperceptible, but they were there, a silent testament to the creature's ancient influence. He pieced together a horrifying picture of a creature that had shaped the city's history, its influence woven into the very fabric of Salt Lake City's existence.

His research uncovered a series of cryptic symbols etched into the old city maps and building blueprints. These symbols, unfamiliar and unsettling, seemed to depict a ritualistic process, a means of containing or channeling the creature's power. He realized that these symbols weren't just ancient markings; they were instructions, a hidden key to understanding and perhaps even controlling the entity. The symbols seemed to respond to him, their lines and curves resonating with the obsidian shards he'd found at the construction site.

He ventured into the city's forgotten tunnels, a network of subterranean passages running beneath the city streets, a labyrinth of shadows and echoing silence. These tunnels, Mike discovered, were the arteries through which the entity's energy flowed, connecting the ley line nodes and amplifying its influence. The air in the tunnels was heavy with the scent of ozone and damp earth, a chilling reminder of the creature's presence. He followed the tunnels, guided by the cryptic symbols, until he reached a vast cavern deep beneath the city's heart.

In the center of the cavern, he found it – a massive obsidian monolith, pulsating with a sinister energy, the source of the city's growing fear. The monolith was covered in the same cryptic symbols he'd found on the maps and blueprints, a testament to its ancient power. As he touched the monolith, a wave of energy surged through him, visions flooding his mind – images of the entity's past, its terrifying power, and the ritual that had bound it to the city. The visions were overwhelming, terrifying, but they also provided him with a crucial piece of information – a way to break the creature's hold on the city, a way to sever its connection to the ley lines and banish it back to the abyss from whence it came. The whispers in the city intensified, a chorus of fear and despair echoing through the cavern. But Mike stood firm, his resolve unwavering. He was ready. The final battle for Salt Lake City was about to begin. The fight was not only for the city, but for the sanity of its inhabitants and, perhaps, for Mike's own soul.

The hum of Ralph's server room was a constant, low thrum against the backdrop of Salt Lake City's growing unease. He hadn't slept properly in days, the flickering screens casting an eerie green glow on his increasingly haggard face. While Mike plunged into the city's shadowy underbelly, Ralph delved into the digital labyrinth, his fingers flying across the keyboard, a symphony of clicks and whirs accompanying his relentless pursuit of answers. The obsidian shards, samples of which Mike had carefully secured and sent to him, remained a baffling enigma. Standard spectral analysis revealed nothing unusual; they were composed of a remarkably pure form of obsidian, yet they pulsed with a faint, almost imperceptible energy that defied conventional scientific explanation.

Ralph's expertise lay in bridging the gap between the mundane and the extraordinary, translating the whispers of the supernatural into the language of data. He poured

over geological surveys, seismic readings, and historical weather patterns, searching for correlations, for anything that might explain the strange energy emanating from the shards and the city's ley lines. He cross-referenced his findings with Venga's cryptic notes, her ancient texts hinting at forgotten rituals and powerful entities bound to the earth's energy currents. Venga's annotations, often in a language Ralph barely understood, were peppered with symbols that mirrored the markings on the obsidian shards, hinting at a long-forgotten connection between the artifacts and the city's ley lines.

His analysis took him down digital rabbit holes, leading him to forgotten archives, obscure online forums dedicated to paranormal activity, and even to the encrypted databases of government agencies. The more he dug, the more he realized the depth and complexity of the threat. The pattern wasn't random; it was intricate, woven into the very fabric of Salt Lake City's history, a dark tapestry of secrets and suppressed truths. The disappearances, the strange occurrences documented in the city's archives, the whispers – they were all connected, bound together by a network of energy that seemed to pulse beneath the city streets.

He mapped the locations of all reported incidents onto a three-dimensional model of the city's subterranean network. The result was breathtaking and terrifying. The incidents weren't scattered randomly; they formed a disturbing pattern, a geometric arrangement that mirrored the configuration of the city's ley lines. The energy emanating from the obsidian shards seemed to intensify whenever he moved the cursor over these specific locations on his model, a tangible manifestation of their connection.

Ralph developed a custom algorithm, feeding it the data points, the seismic readings, and the information from the ancient texts. The algorithm, a complex weave of statistical analysis and pattern recognition, worked tirelessly, sifting through terabytes of data, searching for the slightest anomaly, the faintest hint of a connection. He ran simulations, hypothetical scenarios, exploring every possible explanation, every potential consequence. He worked late into the night, fueled by coffee and the desperate need to understand the entity they were facing.

Days blurred into nights, the lines between his work and his personal life dissolving into a chaotic blend of caffeine-fueled obsession. The weight of the city's fate rested heavily on his shoulders, the responsibility for finding a solution pressing down on him with a crushing force. He was a man of logic, of data, of numbers, yet he found himself facing a challenge that transcended his scientific understanding, a challenge that demanded a different kind of solution.

The algorithm finally yielded a result, a faint but unmistakable pattern emerging from the chaotic data. The ley lines weren't simply conduits of energy; they were resonating chambers, amplifying the power of the entity, feeding its influence into the city's subconscious. The pattern revealed a series of nodes, points of intense energetic activity, corresponding to locations where unexplained events had clustered throughout history. These nodes, Ralph realized, weren't just geographic locations; they were focal points, amplifiers of the entity's power.

One node stood out, far more potent than the others. It lay beneath the city's oldest district, a location that overlapped with the abandoned excavation site Mike had investigated. Ralph's analysis suggested that this particular node was the heart of the problem, the primary source of the entity's influence. It was the epicenter of the resonating network, feeding the energy that was amplifying the whispers, the fear, and the disappearances. This node wasn't merely amplifying the power of the entity; it was sustaining it. Cutting it off would be akin to severing the entity's lifeblood.

He then turned his attention to the obsidian shards, comparing their energy signatures to the energy patterns he'd mapped from the ley lines. He discovered that the shards resonated at a specific frequency, a frequency that corresponded to the activity at the most powerful node. The shards, he theorized, were not merely fragments of some forgotten construction project; they were tuning forks, designed to interact with the ley lines, possibly even to channel or control the entity's energy. This was confirmed by an analysis of the microscopic structure of the shards, revealing intricate carvings far too small to be seen with the naked eye. These carvings, when viewed under a powerful electron microscope, resonated with the same mathematical formulas Ralph had discovered in Venga's texts.

This led to a startling revelation. The entity wasn't just some ancient, malevolent force that had stumbled upon Salt Lake City. It had been deliberately summoned, deliberately bound to the city. A powerful ritual, hinted at in Venga's texts and now mathematically confirmed by Ralph's analysis, had been used to anchor the entity to the city's ley lines, using the obsidian shards as conduits for its power. The ritual, it seemed, hadn't been a one-time event. It was an ongoing process, a constant reinforcement of the entity's hold on Salt Lake City. Ralph's analysis revealed the precise location within the city's oldest district where the core ritual had been performed centuries ago. It was a chilling confirmation of the stories and legends he had dismissed as mere folklore just a few weeks ago.

The realization hit him with the force of a physical blow. The fight wasn't just about destroying an ancient evil; it was about undoing a carefully orchestrated, centuries-old ritual. He knew that Mike needed more than just the location of the node; he needed to understand the nature of the ritual itself, how it worked, and how it could be undone. He compiled his findings into a comprehensive report, a detailed analysis that included the 3D model of the city's energy network, the frequency analysis of the obsidian shards, and a proposed strategy for disrupting the ritual. He sent the report to Mike, knowing the weight of the city, and perhaps the survival of humanity, rested on their next move. The whispers in the city felt louder now, closer, their chilling presence a constant reminder of the looming battle. The clock was ticking.

The air in Venga's small, cluttered apartment hung thick with the scent of incense and old paper. Moonlight, fractured by the stained-glass window depicting a scene of celestial battle, cast long shadows across the room, illuminating shelves laden with ancient texts bound in leather and bone. Dust motes danced in the pale light, creating the illusion of restless spirits. Venga, her face etched with the wisdom – and weariness – of centuries, sat hunched over a table strewn with maps, diagrams, and obsidian shards that pulsed with a faint inner light. She looked like a living embodiment of the city's shadowed history, a conduit between the mundane and the supernatural.

Mike, his face grim and etched with fatigue, leaned against the wall, his gaze fixed on Venga. The previous encounter with Samson had left its mark; a deep scar bisected his left arm, a grim reminder of the fight's ferocity. He'd lost Chet, a loss that gnawed at him, a constant, dull ache in the center of his chest. He needed answers, needed to understand the enemy they faced, not just to defeat him, but to prevent another tragedy.

Venga finally looked up, her eyes, the color of old amber, holding a depth that seemed to contain the weight of ages. "The obsidian," she began, her voice low and resonant, each word carrying the weight of untold stories, "it is not merely a weapon, nor a tool.
It is a key."

She traced a finger across a detailed map of Salt Lake City, a map far older than any Mike had ever seen. The lines etched upon it weren't streets or landmarks; they were shimmering threads of energy, the city's ley lines pulsing with a faint, ethereal glow that seemed to respond to Venga's touch. "These lines," she explained, her voice barely above a whisper, "they are the city's veins, its arteries. They carry the lifeblood of this place, but also… its shadows."

She pointed to a cluster of points marked on the map, points that coincided with the locations Ralph's algorithm had identified as nodes of intense energy. "These points," she continued, "are not merely intersections of energy. They are anchors, focal points where the veil between worlds is thin. Samson… he was drawn to these points, feeding upon the raw power that they channeled."

Mike shifted his weight, a question forming on his lips. "But why Salt Lake City? Why this place?"

Venga sighed, a sound like wind rustling through dead leaves. "This city," she said, "holds a secret, a deep and ancient secret. Centuries ago, a ritual was performed here, a ritual of binding, a summoning."

She picked up one of the obsidian shards, turning it over in her hands. Its surface shimmered with an almost imperceptible light. "These shards," she explained, "were not created naturally. They were crafted, imbued with a power beyond human comprehension. They were designed to be anchors, to amplify the energy of the ley lines, to create a conduit for… something else."

She paused, her gaze distant, lost in the echoes of forgotten times. "The texts… they speak of a being of immense power, a creature bound to this earth, its essence tethered to the city's ley lines. A being that feeds not on blood, but on fear, on despair, on the very essence of human suffering."

Mike leaned closer, his heart pounding a frantic rhythm against his ribs. "Samson… he was serving it?"

Venga nodded, her eyes filled with a chilling certainty. "He was a vessel, a conduit. The ritual didn't create him, but it empowered him, gave him strength beyond his natural capabilities. He was a pawn in a much larger game."

Venga then began to explain the intricacies of the ancient ritual, weaving a tapestry of arcane knowledge and terrifying prophecies. She spoke of forgotten gods and forgotten rituals, of sacrifices made in the darkness, of blood spilled on sacred ground. Her words painted a vivid picture of a dark ceremony conducted centuries ago, a ceremony that had inadvertently opened a gateway to a dimension of pure, unadulterated evil.

She described the ritual's components – the obsidian shards, carved, in detail, with symbols that resonated with the ley lines; the specific locations chosen for their potent energy; the precise timing, dictated by the celestial alignments. She spoke of incantations whispered in a language older than civilization itself, incantations designed to bind the entity to this world, to tether it to Salt Lake City.

The ritual wasn't a one-time event, she explained. It was a sustained effort, a constant reinforcement of the entity's hold on the city. Every act of violence, every moment of fear and despair, served to strengthen the entity's power, feeding it with the city's collective negativity. Samson's actions weren't random; they were part of a larger, terrifying design. He was merely a tool, tasked with gathering the energy needed to maintain the ritual.

Venga's words painted a disturbing picture of a city unknowingly held hostage by an ancient entity, its existence sustained by a ritual that had been perpetuated for centuries. The obsidian shards weren't merely fragments of an ancient artifact; they were resonating keys, tuning forks designed to maintain the flow of energy that sustained the entity.

She revealed that the ritual had been performed in a location within Salt Lake City's oldest district, a place that lay beneath the abandoned excavation site Mike had investigated. This location wasn't simply a nexus of energy; it was the epicenter of the ritual, the heart of the entity's power. It was the source from which the entity drew its strength, its very life force.

The implications were chilling. The fight wasn't simply about defeating Samson; it was about dismantling the centuries-old ritual that had bound the entity to the city. It was a battle against time, against an enemy far more ancient and powerful than they could have ever imagined. The whispers in the city were growing louder, their presence more palpable, a tangible manifestation of the entity's growing power.

Venga's insights offered a chilling yet necessary clarity. They confirmed Ralph's findings, providing the historical and mythological context needed to understand the true nature of their enemy. It wasn't simply about eliminating a vampire; it was about undoing a pact made with oblivion, a pact that threatened to consume Salt Lake City, and perhaps the world, in its darkness. The task ahead loomed, monumental and terrifying, but armed with this new knowledge, Mike felt a spark of resolve ignite within him. The fight was far from over, but now, at least, they knew precisely what they were fighting. They knew their enemy, and they knew what they had to do. The whispers of the city, once a source of fear, now fueled a desperate, burning hope. The hunt would continue.

Chapter 7: The New Enemy

The obsidian shard pulsed faintly in Venga's hand, its surface shimmering with an internal light that seemed to mirror the unsettling calm in her eyes. "The creature," she began, her voice a low thrum that resonated with the ancient power she commanded, "is not what you expect. It's not a physical being, not in the way Samson was. Think… less of a monster, and more of a… corruption."

She leaned forward, her gaze piercing Mike's, "Imagine a shadow, Mike, a shadow that has grown so large, so encompassing, that it has become a being in itself. It feeds not on blood, but on the very fabric of despair. On fear. On the negative energy that humans generate. It thrives in the darkness, in the places where hope dies, where the light cannot reach."

Mike swallowed, the implications heavy and suffocating. He had faced vampires before, creatures of the night with tangible weaknesses, but this... this was something else entirely. Something beyond the realm of simple hunting. This was a battle for the soul of the city.

Venga continued, her voice dropping to a near whisper, "The ritual, as I explained, bound it to this place, to Salt Lake City. But it's not a prison; it's a conduit. The ley lines are not just pathways of energy; they are its veins, its arteries. It draws sustenance from them, from the collective negativity of the city, amplified by the obsidian shards."

She traced the lines on the ancient map, her finger lingering on a specific point beneath the abandoned excavation site. "This place," she said, her voice barely audible, "is not merely the heart of the ritual; it is the heart of the creature itself. It is the nexus point where its influence is strongest, where its presence is most palpable. It's the source of its power. Destroy this point, and you may sever its connection to the city, perhaps even weaken it significantly."

Mike's mind raced, trying to reconcile this nebulous enemy with the concrete reality of the hunt. How do you hunt something that is essentially a sentient shadow, a manifestation of collective despair? How do you even begin to fight it?

"But what are its capabilities?" Mike finally asked, his voice tight with apprehension.

Venga's eyes narrowed, a chilling glint in their depths. "It cannot manifest physically, not directly. It influences individuals, feeds on their negative emotions, twisting their minds, amplifying their fears and insecurities. It can whisper suggestions, plant seeds of doubt and despair, driving people to violence, to madness, to self-destruction."

She paused, then added, with a chilling precision, "Think of Samson, Mike. He wasn't just a vampire; he was a tool, a pawn. The creature amplified his already existing darkness, twisted his desires, controlled his actions. It used him to gather energy, to feed itself. He was a conduit, and when he failed, it would simply find another."

"So, it can possess people?" Ralph asked, his voice laced with apprehension. He'd always been the pragmatist of the group, the one who focused on facts and figures, but even he couldn't deny the terrifying implications of Venga's words.

"Possession is too simplistic," Venga corrected. "It's more of an insidious influence, a subtle manipulation. It doesn't seize control; it corrupts from within. It works through the vulnerabilities of the individual, amplifying their weaknesses, their darkest impulses."

"Then how do we fight it?" Mike pressed, his voice strained. The odds felt insurmountable. They had fought a powerful vampire and lost a comrade. This new threat seemed almost invincible.

"We don't fight it directly," Venga said, her voice surprisingly calm, despite the gravity of the situation. "Not with weapons, not with conventional methods. We sever its connection to the city, its source of power."

"By destroying the ritual site," Ralph interjected.

Venga nodded. "Exactly. That is our priority. We must disrupt the flow of energy, weaken the entity's hold on Salt Lake City. The obsidian shards – they are the keys to the ritual. We need to find the remaining shards, deactivate them, and then destroy the heart of the ritual itself."

She explained that the shards weren't merely scattered; they were strategically placed throughout the city, acting as amplifiers for the entity's power. Finding them would be challenging; they were not ordinary artifacts. Their magical properties allowed them to camouflage themselves, blend in with their surroundings, making them almost impossible to detect without specific knowledge and tools.

"But," she continued, her voice taking on a more serious tone, "destroying the ritual site will not be easy. The entity will defend itself, and it will likely use the city's inhabitants as pawns. It will feed on their fears, their anxieties, turning them against us. We will need to move quickly and decisively. We need a strategy that minimizes civilian casualties."

Venga detailed her plan, a multi-pronged approach that involved a combination of stealth, technological prowess, and ancient magical techniques. She outlined specific procedures for neutralizing the obsidian shards and for disrupting the energy flow at the ritual site. The plan was complex, dangerous, and demanded perfect coordination.

The task ahead was monumental, a fight against a formless enemy that thrived on fear and despair. The hunters were not only fighting for the survival of Salt Lake City, but also for their own sanity, for their ability to remain human in the face of overwhelming evil. The air grew heavy with the weight of the impending battle, the city's whispers intensifying into a terrifying chorus, a prelude to the final, desperate confrontation. The hunt was far from over; it was just beginning. The true battle, for the very soul of Salt Lake City, was about to commence. The hunters prepared themselves, knowing that even with their combined skills and knowledge, success was far from guaranteed. The line between victory and oblivion had never been thinner. The fight was not just against a creature, but against the very essence of despair itself, a battle that would test their limits and push them to the edge of sanity. The city held its breath, unaware of the monstrous threat that lurked beneath, a threat that only a handful of brave souls stood against. The fate of Salt Lake City, and perhaps much more, hung precariously in the balance. The hunt continued.

The flickering gaslight cast long shadows across the worn map spread out on the table, illuminating Venga's intense gaze. "Our previous methods won't work," she stated, her voice low and gravelly, the words echoing the grim reality of their situation. "Samson was a tangible threat, a brute force we could, albeit barely, contend with. This… this is different."

Mike, his jaw tight with grim determination, ran a hand through his already disheveled hair. "Different how?" he asked, his voice strained from exhaustion and the lingering trauma of Chet's death. The memory of Chet's lifeless eyes, wide with shock and disbelief, still haunted him.

Ralph, ever the pragmatist, leaned forward, his brow furrowed in concentration. "Venga mentioned the obsidian shards acting as amplifiers. If we can disable them, we weaken its hold on the city, right?"

Venga nodded. "Precisely. But disabling them is only half the battle. They are not simply scattered haphazardly. They're strategically placed, acting as nodes in a network that channels the city's negative energy to the nexus point. We need to identify and neutralize each shard, then disrupt the flow at its core."

"How do we find them?" Chet's absence loomed large in the room, a palpable void in their usual dynamic. His methodical approach to problem-solving would have been invaluable now.

"The shards aren't easy to spot," Venga explained, her voice laced with a chilling matter-of-factness. "They possess a form of magical camouflage, adapting to their environment. They'll appear as ordinary objects, blending seamlessly into their surroundings. We need to rely on more than just our eyes."

She gestured to a small, intricately carved wooden box she had produced from her satchel. Inside, nestled on a bed of faded velvet, was a collection of strange, almost iridescent stones. "These are resonance stones. They vibrate at a frequency that interacts with the obsidian shards' magical signature. Holding one will allow you to sense their proximity, though it won't pinpoint their exact location. It'll be a guided search, a careful, methodical process."

Mike picked up one of the stones, its surface cool and smooth beneath his fingertips. A faint hum resonated within it, a subtle vibration that seemed to extend into his bones. It felt alien, otherworldly, a palpable connection to the hidden power network beneath the city.

"We'll divide and conquer," Venga proposed, her voice crisp and authoritative. "Ralph, you and I will focus on the downtown area. Mike, you'll take the west side, focusing on older, more established neighborhoods. We'll coordinate via comms, reporting our findings as we locate the shards."

"And what about the nexus point?" Ralph asked, his voice laced with concern. "How do we deal with that?"

"That will be the final phase," Venga replied. "Once we've neutralized the majority of the shards, we'll converge on the abandoned excavation site. We'll need to be prepared for a strong defense. The entity will likely retaliate forcefully when we strike at its heart."

Mike felt a cold dread grip him. They were playing a dangerous game, a deadly chess match against a foe beyond comprehension. Their previous enemy, Samson, had been a terrifying predator, but at least he had been tangible, susceptible to physical attacks. This new entity was an abstract evil, a corruption of the city's soul itself.

"We need a distraction," Mike said, his voice low. "Something to draw its attention away from the nexus point while we're neutralizing the shards."

Ralph nodded. "A decoy, of sorts. But what could possibly draw its attention away from its energy source?"

Venga closed her eyes, her lips moving in silent prayer or incantation. After a moment, she opened them, a glint of calculated ruthlessness in their depths. "We will use the city's own fear against it," she stated, her voice chillingly calm. "We'll create a controlled surge of negative energy, a localized distortion in the city's emotional landscape. It will be drawn to it, its attention diverted."

"How?" Mike asked, intrigued despite the inherent risk.

"Through amplification," Venga explained. "We'll use a combination of technological and magical means to focus and magnify existing negative energy. Think of it as a lure, baiting the creature away from the true target."

She detailed a complex plan involving a network of strategically placed signal amplifiers and specially crafted runes designed to focus and manipulate negative emotions. It was a high-stakes gamble, a potentially dangerous maneuver, but they had little choice. The risk of a direct confrontation at the nexus point without a distraction was simply too high.

"This is a complex operation," Ralph acknowledged, running a hand over his tired eyes. "It requires perfect coordination and timing."

"Indeed," Venga agreed. "Failure is not an option. The fate of Salt Lake City, and possibly more, rests on our success. Prepare yourselves. The hunt begins anew."

The following days were a blur of frantic activity. They worked tirelessly, preparing for the perilous task ahead. Mike, utilizing his technological expertise, set up the amplification network, carefully calibrating the signal emitters to achieve the precise level of negative energy amplification they required. Ralph, using his knowledge of the city's infrastructure, mapped out the optimal placement of the resonance stones, guiding their search for the hidden obsidian shards. Venga, with her arcane knowledge, crafted the runes, imbuing them with potent magical energies capable of manipulating emotional currents.

They worked in near-silence, the weight of their responsibility pressing down on them. The city around them remained blissfully unaware of the monstrous threat lurking beneath, oblivious to the desperate fight brewing in the shadows. Each shard they located felt like a small victory, yet the larger task, the imminent confrontation at the nexus point, cast a long shadow over them. The feeling of dread was palpable, but their determination was unwavering. This time, there would be no retreat. There could only be victory or oblivion. The hunters were ready. The hunt, the final hunt, was about to begin.

The resonance stones, cool and smooth against their skin, hummed a discordant song, a low thrumming that vibrated not just in their hands, but deep within their bones. Mike, guided by the subtle vibrations, traced a path through the labyrinthine streets of Salt Lake City's west side, his footsteps echoing in the pre-dawn stillness. The city, usually a vibrant tapestry of light and noise, was now shrouded in an unnatural quiet, a pregnant silence that spoke of lurking dread. The stone pulsed faster, a frantic heartbeat against his palm, as he approached an old Victorian house, its paint peeling and windows dark. The hum intensified as he neared a seemingly innocuous garden gnome, perched amongst overgrown ivy. The gnome, seemingly ordinary, emitted a faint, almost imperceptible aura of darkness. This was it - an obsidian shard, disguised in plain sight.

Ralph and Venga, meanwhile, navigated the bustling downtown core, their search hampered by the city's daytime clamor. The resonance stones' signals were fainter here, drowned out by the cacophony of human activity. But Venga, with her heightened sensitivity, detected subtle shifts in the ambient energy, imperceptible to the untrained eye. She identified a shard embedded within a seemingly normal street lamp, its magical camouflage skillfully concealing its true nature. The lamp's light flickered erratically, a subtle sign of the shard's presence, a telltale tremor in the city's energy grid. Pulling out a specialized EMF meter, Ralph confirmed the readings. The energy signature was unmistakable: a sharp spike of dark energy, a malevolent pulse in the heart of the city.

Their methodology was a delicate dance between technology and ancient lore. Mike, a former military engineer, relied on his tech prowess, using drones equipped with specialized sensors to scan buildings and underground tunnels, searching for subtle energy anomalies. Ralph, a historian and urban explorer, pieced together clues from old city maps, forgotten chronicles, and local legends, searching for patterns and connections that might reveal the shards' locations. Venga, a practicing shaman with a deep understanding of the city's ley lines, relied on her intuition and mystical senses, sensing the subtle shifts and disturbances in the magical currents. Their combined expertise formed a powerful synergy, allowing them to navigate this intricate, supernatural puzzle.

The information gathered wasn't just about locations; it was about patterns. As they found more shards, they began to discern a horrifying design. The obsidian fragments weren't randomly scattered; they formed a network, a complex web of dark energy that pulsed across the city, feeding into a central point – the abandoned excavation site. The sheer scale of it was staggering, a dark ritual of immense power, a clandestine attempt to corrupt Salt Lake City's very soul.

The excavation site itself was a chilling testament to forgotten history, a gaping wound in the earth that had been abruptly abandoned decades ago. Local legends spoke of strange occurrences, unexplained disappearances, and whispers of a malevolent presence that haunted the area. Now, their investigation confirmed the worst – the site served as a nexus point, the heart of this dark network, the focal point of the entity's power.

The shards weren't merely objects; they were conduits, amplifiers of negative energy, channeling the city's anxieties, fears, and sorrows into a monstrous entity, feeding its malevolent power. Each shard's location was carefully chosen, placed near sites of historical trauma, places where intense negative emotions had been concentrated over time. Abandoned asylums, old cemeteries, forgotten battlegrounds – these were the nodes of the dark network, each shard acting like a malignant parasite, feeding on the city's collective pain.

The realization struck them with chilling force: they weren't simply fighting a monster; they were fighting a corruption, a parasitic entity that had woven itself into the fabric of the city itself. This wasn't merely a physical threat; it was an existential one, a threat to the city's very soul. The stakes were higher than ever before.

Their precise documentation went beyond mere coordinates. They recorded the specific type of energy signature emitted by each shard, noting its intensity and frequency. They documented the surrounding environment, noting any historical significance or unusual energy signatures. Each shard was photographed, in detail, its location carefully mapped using advanced GPS technology. They created a detailed 3D model of the network, visualizing the flow of dark energy, pinpointing critical nodes and potential vulnerabilities. This level of detail was crucial for understanding the enemy, for predicting its reactions, and for formulating a strategy to effectively neutralize it.

Their intelligence gathering wasn't limited to the physical world. Venga, tapping into the city's psychic undercurrents, sensed a palpable sense of dread emanating from the excavation site, a wave of raw, malevolent energy that chilled her to the bone. She described visions of swirling darkness, distorted images of twisted beings, and a sense of suffocating despair, confirming the horrifying nature of the entity they were facing.

The team also delved into the city's archives, poring over forgotten documents, police reports, and historical records, searching for clues about the entity's origins and past activities. They uncovered scattered references to unexplained phenomena, occurrences that were dismissed as coincidence or delusion – until now. The puzzle pieces were beginning to fit together, revealing a terrifying picture of a creature that had been manipulating the city for decades, subtly influencing its history, shaping its destiny.

The next stage involved the creation of their distraction, the controlled surge of negative energy to lure the entity away from the excavation site. Mike and Ralph collaborated, using a combination of strategically placed signal amplifiers and specially designed software. They created a simulated wave of psychic distress, carefully calibrated to mimic the emotional signature that would most effectively attract the entity. Venga, meanwhile, crafted runes of power, amplifying the simulated wave, imbuing it with a potency that would be irresistible to the entity.

The operation was risky, a calculated gamble that relied on precise timing and coordination. One wrong move, one miscalculation, and the city would be at its mercy. But they had no choice. The hunt was entering its final, most perilous phase. The fate of Salt Lake City rested on the precision of their planning, the sharpness of their execution, and their ability to fight an enemy that was not merely a creature, but a corruption of the city itself, a malevolent force woven into the very fabric of its existence. The city slept, unaware of the war being waged in its shadows, a war for its very soul.

The air in Mike's workshop crackled with a nervous energy, a stark contrast to the methodical precision of his movements. He thoroughly calibrated the sensors on a new drone, its sleek, obsidian frame reflecting the harsh fluorescent lights. This wasn't just any drone; it was a custom-built marvel, packed with cutting-edge technology designed to withstand the unpredictable energies they were about to encounter. Its cameras were enhanced with spectral filters, capable of detecting subtle energy shifts invisible to the naked eye. Its processors were fortified against electromagnetic interference, shielding it from the entity's attempts at disruption.

Each wire, each circuit board, had been painstakingly checked, double-checked, and triple-checked. This was their last stand, and failure wasn't an option.

Ralph, meanwhile, hunched over a table laden with ancient texts and arcane symbols, his brow furrowed in concentration. He carefully transcribed passages from a forgotten grimoire, his fingers tracing the faded ink, deciphering cryptic clues left by forgotten scholars. He was painstakingly recreating a protective sigil, a complex arrangement of glyphs designed to deflect the entity's psychic assault. The sigil, woven into a durable, lightweight material, would be attached to each of their tactical vests, providing a crucial layer of protection against the entity's insidious mental attacks. The room was a chaotic blend of modern technology and ancient lore, a testament to the hunters' unusual approach.

Venga sat cross-legged on the floor, her face serene yet intense. She chanted softly, her voice a low, resonant hum that resonated in the confines of the workshop. Around her, a collection of carefully selected herbs and crystals radiated a faint, ethereal glow. She was preparing a potent concoction, a mystical elixir designed to enhance their senses and protect them from the entity's corrupting influence. The air around her shimmered faintly, a subtle indication of the powerful energies she was manipulating. The scent of sandalwood and sage filled the air, a calming counterpoint to the tense atmosphere. This was more than just a physical battle; it was a spiritual one, a clash of wills between good and evil, light and darkness. Her preparations involved more than mere herbs and chants; it was a dance with the spirit world, a careful negotiation with forces beyond human comprehension.

Chet, despite his passing, remained a vital part of their preparations. His detailed notes, his precise analysis of the entity's behavior, formed the backbone of their strategy. Mike constantly referred to Chet's notes, reviewing the energy signatures, studying the patterns of the entity's attacks. His absence was keenly felt, a constant reminder of the sacrifices they were willing to make. The weight of his loss spurred them on, fueling their determination. His death was not in vain; it was a testament to their shared cause and a catalyst for their unrelenting pursuit of justice.

Their preparations extended beyond the physical and spiritual realms. They secured a rooftop vantage point overlooking the excavation site, a location chosen for its strategic advantage and its proximity to the main ley line. Mike, using his military experience, rigged the area with a network of surveillance cameras, motion sensors, and tripwires, creating a sophisticated early warning system. The city below was a tapestry of lights, unaware of the looming threat, of the war being waged in its shadows.

The team carefully reviewed their tactical plan, each member playing a critical role in the upcoming confrontation. Mike would utilize his drones to distract the entity, drawing its attention away from the main assault. Ralph would use his knowledge of the ley lines to disrupt the entity's energy flow, weakening its power. Venga would unleash a wave of pure spiritual energy, a potent counterattack designed to push back the darkness. The coordination, the timing, everything had to be perfect. The slightest error could mean catastrophe.

The weight of their responsibility was immense, a heavy cloak of anticipation settling upon them. They knew they were facing an enemy far more powerful than anything they had encountered before. This wasn't just a monster; it was a corruption, a parasitic entity that had insinuated itself into the very fabric of Salt Lake City, feeding on its fears and anxieties, twisting its soul. They were facing not only physical danger but also a spiritual war, a battle for the city's very essence.

As the city slumbered, they sharpened their weapons, both physical and spiritual. They checked and double-checked their equipment, reinforcing their positions, preparing for the inevitable clash. The atmosphere was thick with tension, a palpable energy that vibrated in the stillness of the night. Their faces were grim, determined, yet a flicker of fear lurked in the depths of their eyes. This was their final chance, their last stand, a battle that would determine not only their fate but the fate of Salt Lake City itself.

The hunters spent hours poring over satellite imagery, studying the excavation site in minute detail. They identified potential weak points in the entity's energy field, areas where their attack might be most effective. They simulated various attack scenarios, anticipating the entity's responses, refining their strategies to maximize their chances of success. The level of detail was obsessive, a testament to their dedication and their understanding of the gravity of the situation.

Their preparations went beyond technology and ancient lore. They had to prepare themselves mentally and emotionally. They meditated, clearing their minds of fear and doubt, focusing their intentions, honing their resolve. They shared stories of their past, strengthening their bonds, reinforcing their loyalty. The unity of their team was their greatest weapon, their unwavering support for one another the shield against despair. This wasn't just a battle for the city; it was a fight for each other, for the life they had chosen, and for the life they had lost.

The city below was oblivious, wrapped in a blanket of quiet. But above, in the shadows, a war was brewing. The hunters prepared, steeling themselves for the ultimate test of their courage, skill, and devotion. The fate of Salt Lake City hung in the balance, suspended on the razor's edge of victory or defeat. The silence was broken only by the rhythmic ticking of a clock, a countdown to the final confrontation, a race against time and against a darkness that threatened to engulf them all. The preparations were complete; the hunt was about to begin.

The obsidian drone, christened "Nightjar" by Mike, hummed quietly in his hands. Its multifaceted lenses, capable of piercing the deepest shadows, reflected the faint glow of the pre-dawn sky. The air hung heavy with a peculiar stillness, a silence so profound it felt almost oppressive. This wasn't the familiar, gritty urban silence of Salt Lake City; this was something else, something… expectant. They were venturing beyond the familiar confines of their previous hunts, venturing into the unknown. The coordinates Ralph had painstakingly gleaned from Chet's final notes led them to the outskirts of the city, a desolate stretch of industrial wasteland bordering the Great Salt Lake.

The location was unnerving. Abandoned factories loomed like skeletal giants against the bruised horizon, their rusted metal groaning under the weight of neglect and the gnawing bite of the wind. A pervasive sense of decay hung in the air, thick and cloying, mingling with the sharp, metallic tang of brine from the nearby lake. It felt less like a place and more like an open wound on the city's skin, a festering sore that had been ignored for too long.

Venga, her face pale and etched with a grim determination, checked the array of protective amulets and talismans she wore. Each piece held a specific purpose, a carefully chosen ward against the unseen horrors that might lurk in this forsaken place. The faint scent of incense, a mixture of myrrh and frankincense, clung to her, a subtle counterpoint to the metallic tang of the air. Her eyes, normally sparkling with an inner light, were clouded with a deep, almost unsettling gravity. She sensed something here, something beyond their current understanding, something ancient and profoundly unsettling.

Ralph, ever the pragmatist, adjusted the frequency on his specialized radio, its antenna stretching toward the unforgiving sky. He was listening for subtle shifts in the electromagnetic field, searching for any hint of the entity's presence, any deviation from the norm. His face, usually animated and full of life, was drawn and tight, reflecting the unspoken apprehension that gnawed at them all. The familiar comfort of ancient texts and arcane symbols offered little solace here; this was a realm beyond the confines of even his extensive knowledge.

Mike, his gaze sweeping across the desolate landscape, felt a chilling premonition. This wasn't Samson Bordeau; this was something different, something older, something far more insidious. The energy signatures Chet had recorded, the subtle shifts in the ley lines, hinted at a power far exceeding anything they had encountered before. This was a threat that challenged not only their physical prowess but also the very essence of their being.

They moved cautiously, their footsteps muffled by the layers of dust and grime that coated the uneven ground. The silence was broken only by the occasional screech of a rusted hinge or the mournful cry of a lone gull circling overhead. The air grew colder, the wind picking up, carrying with it the faintest whisper of something... unnatural. They could almost feel the presence, a pervasive sense of being watched, of being hunted.

Nightjar, the drone, flitted ahead, its silent whir a barely audible whisper in the oppressive stillness. Its cameras, enhanced with infrared and ultraviolet filters, relayed a disconcerting image to Mike's headset. Anomalies appeared on the screen, flickering patterns of energy that seemed to defy explanation. The ground itself seemed to pulse with a dark, malevolent energy, a subterranean tremor that resonated deep within their bones.

They reached a crumbling edifice, once a grand warehouse, now reduced to a hollow shell, its walls scarred with graffiti and ravaged by time. Inside, the darkness was absolute, broken only by the faint, ethereal glow of Venga's protective talismans. The air was thick with the smell of damp earth and something else... something acrid and sickening, a scent that seemed to claw at the back of their throats.

Suddenly, a low growl, guttural and primal, echoed from the depths of the building. The ground trembled beneath their feet, a seismic shudder that sent a jolt of fear through their veins. The air grew thick with a palpable energy, a chilling wave of dread that washed over them, leaving them breathless and paralyzed with fear.

Nightjar's camera feed went haywire, the image flickering wildly, then dissolving into static. Silence descended once more, but this time, it was a silence thick with anticipation, with the promise of something terrible about to unfold. The growl returned, louder this time, closer, accompanied by a sound like the scraping of bone on stone, a sound that chilled them to the marrow.

Ralph's radio crackled to life, a burst of static followed by a voice, distorted and chilling. "You have awakened something that should have remained dormant," the voice hissed, "something that hungers... for souls." The voice was disembodied, ancient, devoid of any human emotion. It was the voice of something ancient and malevolent. Something far beyond their comprehension.

The ground beneath them buckled. A chasm opened up before them, swallowing Nightjar whole. From the darkness below, a shape emerged, huge and monstrous, a creature of shadow and bone, its eyes burning with malevolent light. It was unlike anything they had ever seen, an embodiment of primal fear, a living nightmare given form. The creature let out a deafening roar, and the very air around them crackled with raw, terrifying energy.

They were surrounded, trapped, their weapons useless against this unimaginable horror. The ground trembled, the air crackled, and the city, unaware of the horrors unleashed on its edge, slumbered on. This was not a battle; it was an annihilation. The hunters, hardened veterans of countless battles, felt a primal fear grip their hearts, a fear that transcended the rational and plunged them into the depths of pure, unadulterated terror. Their carefully crafted plan, their thoroughly honed skills, their spiritual preparations, seemed utterly insignificant in the face of this primordial evil.

A haunting image of the monstrous creature, its silhouette looming large against the pre-dawn sky, its eyes burning into their very souls. The hunters stood frozen, paralyzed by terror and overwhelmed by the raw power of this new enemy. The fight for Salt Lake City was far from over, and the fate of the city, and perhaps the world, hung precariously in the balance. The air crackled, the ground rumbled, and the ancient, forgotten evil rose to claim its due. The hunters braced themselves, knowing that the battle for survival had just begun, and that the true horror was yet to come. The unknown had revealed itself, and it was far more terrifying than any of them could have ever imagined.

Chapter 8: A New Battle

The creature lunged, a blur of shadow and bone, its claws raking across the cracked earth, sending up geysers of dust and debris. Mike reacted instantly, his combat instincts honed over years of facing down the undead, throwing himself to the side, narrowly avoiding the creature's devastating strike. The air vibrated with the force of the impact, a shockwave that sent shivers down their spines. The ground cracked further, widening the chasm that had swallowed Nightjar, its metallic shriek echoing eerily in the cavernous space.

Venga, chanting a protective incantation in a guttural tongue, raised her hand, unleashing a wave of shimmering, emerald energy. The energy struck the creature, causing it to recoil, its shadow-like form flickering momentarily as if struck by lightning. But the effect was fleeting. The creature, impossibly resilient, shook off the energy blast as if it were a mere annoyance. Its roar echoed through the desolate landscape, a sound that spoke of ages of slumber and a hunger that had been awakened, a hunger that could only be satiated with blood and souls.

Ralph, ever sensible even in the face of utter annihilation, fired his custom-made pulse rifle, a weapon designed to disrupt the electromagnetic fields that sustained many supernatural beings. The weapon discharged a concentrated blast of energy, a searing bolt that struck the creature's chest. The impact caused a ripple of distortion in the air, but the creature remained largely unscathed, its shadowy form shimmering as if it were merely passing through the weapon's energy.

Chet's death echoed in Mike's mind. The loss weighed heavy on him, fueling his rage and determination. Chet's final notes, painstakingly deciphered by Ralph, had led them to this desolate place, this ancient evil. The creature before them, a being far exceeding the power of Samson Bordeau, surpassed even Mike's grim expectations. This was no ordinary vampire, no simple creature of the night. This was something older, something more primal, something that belonged to the dawn of time itself. This was a creature born from the dark heart of the earth, fueled by the ancient energies of the ley lines.

The creature advanced, its movements surprisingly agile despite its massive size. Its skeletal frame, a gruesome tapestry of bone and shadow, moved with terrifying speed. Each step sent tremors through the ground, each breath a gust of chilling wind. Its eyes, glowing with an infernal light, were fixed upon them, promising only pain and oblivion.

Mike, drawing his silver-plated katana – a weapon blessed by Venga – charged, his movements a blur of precise strikes. The blade sliced through the creature's shadowy form, but the impact produced only a metallic clang and a faint spark. The creature wasn't flesh and blood; it was something else, something far more ancient and resistant to conventional means of destruction.

Venga continued her incantations, her voice rising above the creature's roars, weaving a complex web of protection around the team. Her amulets glowed with an intense light, radiating protective energy that deflected some of the creature's attacks. But even her powerful magic felt strained, threatened by the overwhelming power of the ancient being. Her chants, once rhythmic and confident, now held a note of desperation, a testament to the immense power they faced.

Ralph, reloading his pulse rifle, switched to a different frequency, aiming for the creature's core, the unseen heart that pulsed with dark energy. He fired another blast, the energy impacting the creature's torso. This time, the effect was slightly more pronounced. A wave of energy rippled through the creature, causing it to momentarily stumble, a brief sign of weakness in its otherwise terrifying strength.

The battle raged on, a chaotic dance of destruction and desperation. Mike's katana flashed, Ralph's pulse rifle roared, and Venga's protective magic shimmered and surged. But the creature was relentless, its attacks growing more ferocious, its power seemingly boundless. Its roars shook the ground, its claws tore at the earth, and its shadow-like form writhed with a malevolent energy that threatened to consume them all.

The hunters fought with a grim determination, their skills and experience tested to their limits. They were outnumbered, outmatched, and facing an enemy beyond their comprehension. Yet, they fought on, driven by a fierce loyalty to each other and a desperate need to protect Salt Lake City from the ancient evil that had been awakened. Their battle was a testament to the human spirit, a display of courage and resilience in the face of overwhelming odds.

The fight continued for what felt like an eternity. They moved between crumbling concrete, dodging the creature's monstrous blows, their strength waning, their hopes dwindling. Each strike, each blast, each incantation felt increasingly futile. The air was thick with the scent of ozone and the metallic tang of blood – a mix of the creature's essence and their own wounds.

As the battle wore on, a chilling realization dawned upon them. This creature wasn't just powerful; it was ancient, a guardian of this forgotten place, a being linked inextricably to the very ley lines that ran beneath Salt Lake City. To defeat it, they needed to understand its connection to the city, its ties to the earth, its source of power. They needed a strategy beyond brute force, a plan that could exploit its vulnerabilities, its ties to this desolate, forgotten place.

A desperate hope flickered within Mike. He remembered Chet's final words, a whispered fragment of a forgotten ritual, a way to sever the creature's connection to the ley lines, a way to starve it of its power. But the ritual was incomplete, shrouded in cryptic symbolism and obscure references. They needed to decipher it, interpret its meaning, and execute it flawlessly, before their own strength gave way to the creature's unrelenting might.

The creature roared again, its shadow-like form looming over them, a terrifying presence that threatened to engulf them completely. Yet, amidst the chaos and desperation, a spark of defiance ignited within them. They were hunters, protectors, warriors against the darkness. They would not surrender, they would not give in. They would fight to the very end, for the sake of Salt Lake City, for the memory of Chet, and for the hope of a future free from this ancient, malevolent terror.

The confrontation was far from over. The hunters, battered and bruised, were on the verge of exhaustion, yet they clung to a sliver of hope, a desperate plan forming in Mike's mind, based on Chet's cryptic notes and his own growing understanding of the creature's connection to the land. The battle was a brutal dance of shadow and steel, an agonizing struggle against a foe beyond any they had ever imagined. But the hunters, bound by their shared experience and unwavering resolve, fought on, their hearts pounding, their breath ragged, their wills forged in the crucible of this desperate, impossible fight. The fate of Salt Lake City, and perhaps much more, hung in the balance.

The creature's next attack was a whirlwind of shadow and bone. It spun with impossible speed, its shadowy limbs blurring into a vortex of darkness, each strike aimed with chilling precision. Mike barely managed to parry a blow that would have cleaved him in two, the force of the impact sending jolts up his arms, nearly dislodging his katana. Ralph, firing rapidly, managed to disrupt the creature's momentum momentarily, but the effect was minimal. The pulse rifle's energy merely seemed to ripple across the creature's surface, like pebbles skipping across water. Venga, her face pale with exertion, continued to weave her protective spells, her chants a desperate plea against the encroaching darkness. Her amulets, usually vibrant and glowing, were dimming, their protective energies strained to their breaking point.

This wasn't just a fight; it was a struggle against the very fabric of the earth itself. The creature was an embodiment of the ley lines, its power drawn from the ancient energies that pulsed beneath Salt Lake City. Every blow, every roar, was a manifestation of that raw, untamed force. The hunters, despite their years of experience, were facing an enemy that defied their understanding, an enemy that seemed to draw strength from the very ground beneath their feet.

A crack ran across the earth, splitting the ground near Venga's feet. She stumbled, her concentration breaking for a fraction of a second. The creature seized the opportunity, its shadowy claws reaching out, aiming for her throat. Mike, reacting instinctively, hurled himself forward, his katana intercepting the attack. The impact sent a shockwave through his body, the force nearly throwing him off his feet. He rolled away, his ears ringing, his body screaming in protest.

Ralph, seeing the opening, switched tactics. He tossed a specially designed grenade – a concoction of holy water, silver dust, and a potent electromagnetic pulse – aiming for a point where the creature's shadowy form seemed to coalesce, a point that Mike suspected might be its core. The grenade exploded with a deafening roar, sending out a wave of blinding light and a shockwave that sent the creature reeling. For a moment, it stumbled, its movements becoming sluggish, its roars reduced to pained hisses.

It was a fleeting moment, a mere reprieve in the face of overwhelming odds. The creature, regaining its composure, roared its fury, its shadowed form writhing with renewed energy. It lunged again, its attacks even more ferocious than before. The hunters, battered and bruised, fought back with grim determination. But their strength was waning, their hopes diminishing. They were fighting against an ancient evil, a guardian of the earth, a being intimately connected to the very heart of Salt Lake City.

Mike, gasping for breath, looked around. The landscape around them had been ravaged by the battle. The once-desolate cavern was now a scene of utter destruction, the earth torn apart, the air thick with the smell of ozone and the metallic tang of blood. He saw Ralph, reloading his pulse rifle with trembling hands. Venga, despite her earlier stumble, held her ground, continuing to weave her protective magic, her face etched with grim determination.

Suddenly, Mike noticed something: a faint shimmering in the earth, emanating from a crack that had opened near where the creature's most recent impact had landed. It was a faint pulsating light, a subtle energy emanating from the ley lines themselves. It was as if the creature's attacks had weakened the barriers between the earthly plane and the raw, untamed power of the ley lines.

A plan began to take shape in his mind. He remembered Chet's fragmented notes, the references to an ancient ritual, a way to disrupt the creature's connection to the ley lines, to starve it of its power. He'd dismissed it earlier, viewing it as a desperate long shot. Now, seeing the glowing crack in the earth, he felt a surge of hope, a sense that Chet's cryptic clues might be more than just riddles, that they held the key to their survival.

He relayed his plan to Ralph and Venga. Ralph, ever the pragmatist, remained skeptical but agreed to help. Venga, her face grim but resolute, nodded in assent. Their battle had reached a critical point, and they had to act quickly, decisively. The creature, recovering fully, unleashed another wave of attacks, its shadowy form a maelstrom of bone and darkness. But this time, the hunters weren't just fighting to survive; they were fighting with a new purpose, a new strategy based on the unexpected discovery of the weakened ley lines and the hope offered by Chet's fragmented ritual.

The execution of Chet's ritual proved to be more challenging than they'd anticipated. The cryptic notes were filled with symbolism and obscure references, demanding a level of understanding that pushed their limits. The ritual required a precise orchestration of their combined skills, blending Venga's knowledge of ancient languages and mystical practices with Ralph's technical expertise in manipulating electromagnetic fields and Mike's understanding of the creature's unique vulnerabilities.

As they performed the ritual, the air crackled with an unnatural energy, the earth beneath them vibrating with the ancient power of the ley lines. The creature, sensing the shift in the balance of power, roared in rage, its attacks becoming even more frenzied. The battle intensified, the hunters performing their ritual amid a hail of shadowy claws and bone-shattering blows. Every second felt like an eternity, each move a gamble between life and death.

As they reached the culminating moment of the ritual, an energy surge erupted, the combined might of Venga's magic and Ralph's technological prowess unleashed with pinpoint accuracy. A blinding flash of emerald light struck the earth near the glowing crack, targeting the creature's unseen connection to the ley lines. The air vibrated violently, the ground bucked and trembled. The creature let out a piercing shriek, a sound of agonizing pain and profound defeat. Its shadowy form began to flicker, its power waning, its form dissolving into the very earth from which it had emerged. The ancient evil, the guardian of the ley lines, was finally weakening, its connection to this world severed. The hunters, exhausted but triumphant, stood their ground, watching as the creature's shadowy form dissipated entirely, leaving only silence and the lingering scent of ozone.

The battle was far from over. The final blow, they knew, was yet to come. But for now, they had found a way to sever the monster's power. The land seemed to sigh in relief, as if a heavy burden had been lifted. The hunters, battered, bleeding, and exhausted, stood side-by-side, a testament to their resilience and unwavering commitment to their mission. The immediate danger was past, but the fight to protect Salt Lake City, they knew, was far from over.

The silence that followed the creature's demise was heavy, thick with the lingering scent of ozone and the metallic tang of blood. It wasn't the triumphant silence of victory, but rather a tense, expectant quiet. The earth, still trembling from the aftershocks of the ritual, seemed to hold its breath. Mike, Ralph, and Venga stood amidst the devastation, their bodies aching, their minds reeling from the intensity of the battle. They had won a crucial battle, but the war was far from over.

Venga, her face pale and drawn, sank to her knees, her hands clasped tightly together. The strain of the ritual had taken its toll, leaving her weak and trembling. Her usually vibrant amulets, now dull and lifeless, hung limply around her neck, testament to the immense energy she had expended. Ralph, ever the pragmatist, began thoroughly checking his pulse rifle, his movements slow and deliberate, his face etched with fatigue. The battle had severely depleted their ammunition, and he needed to assess their remaining resources carefully. Mike, despite the throbbing pain in his arms and the deep gash across his leg, felt a surge of grim determination. He knew that their respite would be short-lived.

The cavern, once a desolate expanse of rock and shadow, was now a chaotic landscape of shattered stone and twisted metal. The ground was cracked and scarred, a testament to the raw power unleashed during the confrontation. They had fought on sacred ground, a place where the earth's energy pulsed with ancient power, and the scars of their battle would remain long after the memory of the creature faded. As they surveyed the damage, a creeping dread began to settle over them. The creature's defeat had been pyrrhic; they had paid a heavy price for their victory. They had survived, but at what cost?

A chilling realization dawned on Mike. The creature's defeat hadn't resolved the underlying problem. They had merely severed its connection to the ley lines, weakening it but not destroying it completely. The source of the evil, the deeper corruption within the city's energy, remained. He knew, instinctively, that this was just the beginning, a prelude to a larger, more terrifying confrontation. The whispers of the ancient texts, previously dismissed as mere folklore, now echoed in his mind with chilling clarity.

He remembered Chet's warnings, his frantic scrawls in his journal, the cryptic references to a greater entity, a shadowy being that resided deep within the heart of Salt Lake City, drawing power from the city's very essence. Chet had sensed a deeper threat, a malevolent force that had been manipulating events, using Samson Bordeau as a pawn in its larger, more sinister game. His death had been a sacrifice, a calculated move to buy time, to give the others a chance to prepare for the inevitable.

The weight of responsibility pressed down on Mike's shoulders. He was the leader, the one who had to make the difficult decisions, the one who had to guide his remaining companions through the darkness that loomed ahead. He had to face the truth: they weren't fighting just one monster; they were fighting against a vast, insidious evil that was deeply entrenched in the city's very soul. The fight for Salt Lake City was far from over, and he had to figure out how to confront the greater threat.

Ralph, breaking the silence, pointed to a faint shimmer emanating from one of the deeper cracks in the earth. It was a pulsating emerald light, subtly different from the earlier glow, far more intense and focused. It pulsed with an eerie rhythm, radiating an energy that was both terrifying and strangely beautiful. Venga, slowly rising to her feet, recognized it instantly. "The heart," she whispered, her voice barely audible above the wind whistling through the cavern. "The heart of the ley lines is exposed. The creature's connection… it severed a protective layer. Now, something far worse is within reach."

The weight of her words settled heavily upon the hunters. They had defeated one monster, only to find themselves on the brink of confronting something far greater, something far more ancient and terrifying. The creature they had vanquished had been a guardian, a protector of sorts, shielding them from a deeper, darker evil that had now become exposed. Their victory, it seemed, had come at a terrible price.

The next few hours were spent in tense planning and preparation. They gathered the remaining supplies, carefully rationing their ammunition and healing salves. Venga, despite her exhaustion, carefully cleansed and recharged her remaining amulets, whispering ancient incantations in a low, urgent tone. Ralph repaired his pulse rifle, his movements precise and efficient, his face reflecting a grim resolve. Mike studied Chet's notes again, focusing on the cryptic passages that hinted at the greater threat and the methods needed to face it.

As daylight crept into the ravaged cavern, casting long, eerie shadows, the hunters emerged, their faces grim and determined. The city awaited them, its beauty masked by the encroaching darkness, its hidden heart pulsating with an ominous energy. They knew they were facing a foe beyond their comprehension, a threat that could engulf Salt Lake City in an unimaginable nightmare. But they also knew they couldn't abandon the city to its fate. They were its protectors, its last line of defense against an ancient evil that was far more powerful, and far more insidious than anything they had ever encountered.

Their next steps were fraught with danger. The city itself felt different, a palpable sense of unease hanging in the air. The usual bustle of city life felt muted, replaced by a strange quiet, punctuated only by the distant wail of sirens. They moved through the deserted streets, their senses on high alert, their weapons ready. Every shadow seemed to writhe with malevolent intent, every whisper of the wind carried a foreboding message.

They knew the risk they were taking. The heart of the ley lines, now exposed, was a beacon of power, both for them and for the lurking evil. They would need to use Chet's fragmented ritual again, but this time, on a larger scale, a more ambitious scale that risked unleashing forces beyond their control. Their only hope lay in understanding the intricate dance between the city's ley lines and the ancient evil that now threatened to consume it. The fight for Salt Lake City had reached its climax. The final battle was upon them, and the odds were stacked against them, but they were ready to face whatever lay ahead. The fate of Salt Lake City rested on their shoulders, their courage, and the desperate hope that their sacrifice would be enough. The city, the ley lines, and the very fabric of reality itself trembled on the brink of destruction.

The emerald light pulsed, a malevolent heartbeat in the city's underbelly. It throbbed with an intensity that resonated not just in the cavern, but seemingly throughout Salt Lake City itself. The air crackled with an unnatural energy, a tangible tension that pressed down on the hunters, weighing on their already burdened souls. Venga, her face etched with a grim determination that belied her exhaustion, began to chant. Her voice, usually a melodious counterpoint to the city's rhythm, was now a low, guttural drone, a desperate plea woven into ancient syllables. The words, a forgotten language passed down through generations of her family, vibrated with a power that felt both ancient and terrifyingly modern.

Ralph, his eyes narrowed in concentration, calibrated his pulse rifle, its mechanisms humming with a faint, almost inaudible whine. He adjusted the targeting system, his movements precise and fluid, the result of years spent honing his skills in the shadowed corners of the city's underworld. He wasn't just fighting a monster; he was fighting against an unseen force that threatened to unravel the very fabric of their reality. The weight of responsibility, the knowledge that the fate of countless lives rested on his shoulders, fueled his grim resolve.

Mike, his leg throbbing with pain, studied Chet's notes once more, the faded ink seeming to blur under the flickering emerald light. Chet's last frantic scrawls, his desperate attempts to convey a message that was beyond words, spoke of a ritual, a complex weave of energy and incantation designed to counteract the malevolent force at the heart of the ley lines. But the notes were incomplete, fragmented, hinting at a knowledge that Chet himself hadn't fully grasped. Mike knew they were venturing into uncharted territory, a realm where the line between reality and the supernatural was blurred beyond recognition.

As Venga's chanting reached a crescendo, the emerald light intensified, expanding outwards, its energy rippling through the cavern like seismic waves. The air thrummed with power, a raw, untamed force that threatened to overwhelm them. The ground beneath their feet trembled, the very earth seeming to shudder under the strain of the unleashed energy. Suddenly, a deep, guttural roar echoed through the cavern, a sound that seemed to emanate from the very depths of the earth, a sound that chilled them to the bone.

From the heart of the ley lines, a shadowy figure emerged, its form shifting and swirling like smoke, its features obscured by an impenetrable darkness. It was vast and terrifying, a being of pure shadow, its very presence exuding an aura of malevolent power. It was far more than just a creature; it was an embodiment of chaos, an ancient entity that had dwelled in the city's heart for centuries, feeding off its energy, manipulating its inhabitants.

This was the true source of the evil, the being that had orchestrated the fog-vampire attacks, using Samson Bordeau as a pawn in its sinister game. It was a force that transcended the limitations of mortal understanding, a being that existed outside the confines of space and time. Its eyes, when they finally became visible, burned with an icy fire, devoid of compassion or mercy.

The battle was not fought with bullets or blades but with the raw power of will, a clash of ancient energies. Venga's chanting intensified, her amulets glowing with a fierce, protective light. Ralph unleashed a barrage of pulse rifle fire, the energy blasts striking the shadowy entity but failing to inflict lasting damage. The being absorbed the blasts, its form flickering momentarily before reforming, its power seemingly undiminished.

Mike, recognizing the futility of direct confrontation, focused on Chet's ritual, his fingers dancing across the worn pages of the journal, his mind struggling to decipher the fragmented instructions. He realized the ritual wasn't meant to destroy the entity but to redirect its energy, to sever its connection to the city's ley lines and banish it back to the abyss from whence it came. The ritual was a precarious dance, a delicate balance of energy flows, requiring precise timing and unwavering focus.

The shadowy entity attacked with a ferocity that bordered on madness. It unleashed tendrils of shadow, attempting to ensnare the hunters, to drain their energy and break their will. Ralph fell, his pulse rifle clattering to the ground, a tendril of shadow seizing him, draining the life from his body. Venga, her voice strained, continued her chant, her energy failing, her amulets dimming.

Mike, realizing time was running out, pushed himself to the limit, his mind racing, his fingers flying across the pages of Chet's journal. He pieced together the fragmented instructions, his understanding of the ritual growing clearer with each passing moment. He channeled his own energy, drawing upon the strength of his resolve, the fierce loyalty to his fallen companions, and the desperate hope of saving Salt Lake City.

He channeled the remaining energy from Venga's depleted amulets, weaving them into the ritual, amplifying its power. With a final, desperate surge of energy, he completed the ritual, his body trembling, his mind teetering on the brink of collapse. The cavern was engulfed in a blinding light, a vortex of energy spinning out of control. The shadowy entity roared, its form convulsing as the ritual's energy tore at its essence.

The vortex intensified, pulling the entity towards its heart, draining its power, tearing its form apart. Slowly, agonizingly, the shadowy being was banished, sucked back into the abyss from which it had come. The emerald light faded, leaving behind a silence heavy with the weight of the battle fought and won. The cavern was silent, except for the faint whisper of the wind and the soft sob escaping Venga's lips.

The cost had been immense. Ralph was gone, his sacrifice a testament to his loyalty and courage. Venga was near collapse, her body drained of energy. Mike, his mind and body ravaged, stood amidst the wreckage, the weight of the world resting heavily upon his shoulders. They had saved Salt Lake City, but at a terrible price. The city remained, its heart battered but still beating, its future uncertain but not yet lost. The hunters had won a brutal war, but they knew, deep in their hearts, that the fight for the city, for humanity itself, was far from over. The victory was pyrrhic, a testament to their resilience, a warning of the darkness that still lurked in the shadows, waiting for its opportunity to strike again. The battle had ended, but the war had just begun.

The vortex of energy, born from Mike's desperate invocation of Chet's incomplete ritual, pulsed with an almost unbearable intensity. It wasn't merely light; it was a living, breathing entity, a chaotic maelstrom of raw power that threatened to tear the very fabric of the cavern apart. The air crackled and hissed, the smell of ozone sharp in their nostrils, a tangible manifestation of the cosmic forces at play. Venga, her body wracked with exhaustion, slumped against a jagged rock, her chanting reduced to a choked whisper, her protective amulets glowing with a faint, flickering light, like dying embers in the heart of a storm.

The shadowy entity, the ancient being that had orchestrated the city's nightmare, reacted with primal rage. It was no longer the subtly manipulative force they had faced earlier; now, it was a creature of pure, unadulterated malice, its form thrashing wildly within the vortex, its shadowy tendrils lashing out with desperate fury. The cavern walls seemed to tremble under the assault, dust and debris raining down from the ceiling as if the very earth itself recoiled in terror from the clash of titanic forces.

Mike, his body trembling from the sheer exertion of the ritual, staggered back, his vision blurring, his ears ringing with the cacophony of the elemental battle. He had pushed himself beyond his limits, beyond the threshold of human endurance, his very essence stretched taut, ready to snap at any moment. He clung to consciousness by a thread, his mind a whirlwind of fragmented thoughts and memories, his body screaming in protest against the unbearable strain.

The entity's roars echoed through the cavern, a symphony of pain and rage, each sound a physical blow that reverberated through Mike's very bones. He could feel the being's malevolent will, a tide of pure darkness pressing against his own, attempting to break his resolve, to shatter his spirit and claim his soul. But Mike held fast, fueled by a fierce determination, a stubborn refusal to surrender. He was not merely fighting for himself, or even for his fallen comrades; he was fighting for the city, for the innocent lives caught in the crossfire of this cosmic war.

Suddenly, a shift in the vortex's energy. The maelstrom, instead of continuing its chaotic dance, began to coalesce, to organize itself. The blinding light intensified, becoming almost unbearable, forcing Mike to shield his eyes. A piercing shriek, filled with unimaginable agony, ripped through the cavern, a sound that seemed to claw at the very soul. Then, silence. A profound, deafening silence, broken only by the ragged gasps of Venga and the rhythmic thump-thump-thump of Mike's own heart, a frantic drumbeat against the backdrop of an unnatural stillness.

Slowly, cautiously, Mike lowered his hand, peering into the heart of the now-calmer vortex. The emerald light had faded, replaced by a soft, ethereal glow. The shadowy entity was gone. The cavern, previously filled with the oppressive weight of its presence, felt strangely empty, hollowed out, as if a vast void had been created in its wake. The raw, chaotic energy that had permeated the air had dissipated, leaving behind an unsettling quietude, the kind of silence that precedes a storm, or perhaps, the aftermath of one.

Venga, her face pale and drawn, slowly opened her eyes. She looked around the cavern, her gaze lingering on the spot where the shadowy entity had been. Her eyes, usually sparkling with a fierce intelligence, were now filled with a haunting emptiness, a reflection of the immense toll the battle had taken. She reached out a trembling hand, touching the spot where Ralph had fallen, her fingers tracing the outline of the bloodstain on the cold, damp stone.

Mike knelt beside her, his own body aching, his mind reeling from the strain of the ritual. He placed a hand on her shoulder, offering a silent comfort, a shared understanding of the sacrifice they had made, the price they had paid for the city's salvation. The victory was bittersweet, a hard-won triumph purchased with the life of a friend, a comrade, a brother in arms. The weight of their loss settled upon them, a crushing burden that threatened to crush their spirits.

They sat there for a long time, in the echoing silence of the cavern, the only sound the gentle drip of water from the stalactites above. The silence was a stark contrast to the maelstrom of energy that had preceded it, a testament to the intensity of the battle, the enormity of the victory. But even in the silence, they could feel the echoes of the battle reverberating through their bodies, through their minds, through their very souls.

The air still held a faint trace of ozone, a lingering reminder of the cosmic forces they had confronted. The cavern, once a place of darkness and dread, now felt different, strangely cleansed, as if the ancient entity's expulsion had somehow purged it of its malevolent influence. Yet, the feeling of emptiness persisted, a void that mirrored the one in their hearts, the absence of their fallen comrade. The fight was over, but the sorrow lingered, a heavy shroud draped over their hard-won victory.

As they slowly made their way out of the cavern, emerging into the cool night air of Salt Lake City, the city itself seemed to breathe a collective sigh of relief. The oppressive weight that had settled over it for so long seemed to lift, replaced by a sense of cautious optimism. But the hunters knew that the respite would be short-lived. The victory was pyrrhic, a temporary reprieve in a war that was far from over. The shadowy entity might be gone, but the forces of darkness remained, lurking in the shadows, waiting for their moment to strike again. The city was safe, for now, but the battle had only just begun. The hunters, scarred and weary but unbroken, stood on the precipice of a new and unknown struggle, their resolve tempered by loss, their determination fueled by the memory of their fallen comrade. The night held no comfort, only the grim promise of more battles to come, more sacrifices to be made. The fight was far from over. The war had just begun. And they, the weary hunters, were ready.

Chapter 9: Resolution and Renewal

The cavern mouth yawned before them, a gaping maw spitting them back into the chilling Salt Lake City night. The air, though cleansed of the oppressive aura of the ancient entity, still carried the metallic tang of blood and the lingering scent of ozone. Venga, her face ashen, leaned heavily on Mike, her breaths shallow and ragged. The silence of their victory pressed down on them, heavier than the oppressive weight of the entity's presence had ever been.

Their victory was a hollow echo in the vast emptiness of their grief. Chet was gone, his sacrifice a brutal price paid for the city's salvation. The weight of their loss felt tangible, a physical burden pressing down on their shoulders, threatening to crush them beneath its weight. They had vanquished a cosmic horror, but they had also lost a piece of themselves, a piece they knew could never be replaced.

The city, however, seemed oblivious to their sorrow. The fog that had clung to the streets like a shroud for weeks was lifting, revealing a sky dusted with the faintest hint of dawn. The usual city sounds – the distant rumble of traffic, the chatter of voices – were a stark contrast to the deathly silence of the cavern they had just left. Yet, the quiet hum of the city held a new note, a subtle undercurrent of relief, a collective sigh of gratitude for the respite from the unseen terror that had stalked their streets.

But the respite was fragile, temporary. They knew it. The fight against the darkness wasn't over; it had merely shifted. The ancient entity, the orchestrator of their nightmare, might be gone, but its influence, its legacy, lingered. The city was safe, for now, but the seeds of fear, the shadows of uncertainty, remained. A new threat, perhaps even more insidious, more dangerous, awaited them.

The revelation of Samson Bordeau's connection to the city's ley lines had sent shivers down their spines. They had initially tracked him as a lone, ravenous predator, but his connection to the city's energy flows hinted at a larger, more sinister presence at work. He wasn't simply a rogue vampire; he was a pawn, a tool, a manifestation of something far greater. And now, with the entity gone, the question remained: who or what would take its place?

The hunt for Samson began anew, not in the dark, claustrophobic depths of a hidden cavern, but on the treacherous rooftops and shadowy alleyways of Salt Lake City. The hunters, armed with their knowledge of the city's ley lines and the ancient texts Chet had painstakingly deciphered, moved like phantoms in the pre-dawn gloom. Their movements were fluid, precise, honed by years of experience and tempered by the recent loss.

The chase led them across a labyrinthine cityscape, a dizzying dance of pursuit and evasion. Samson, weakened but far from defeated, was a shadow flitting across the rooftops, a ghost moving through the urban landscape. He was quicker, stronger, more desperate now, fighting for survival, fueled by a primal instinct to escape. The hunters, relentless in their pursuit, used every technological advantage at their disposal, their drones buzzing like angry hornets above the city's skyline, their thermal imaging cameras piercing the darkness, tracking the vampire's trail of chilling heat signatures.

The first encounter was a brutal ballet of violence and evasion, played out on the precarious edge of a skyscraper.

Samson, his eyes burning with a cold, unnatural light, attacked with a ferocity born of desperation. Mike, his movements precise and economical, parried the vampire's attacks with a skill honed by years of training, his every move a calculated response. Venga, despite her exhaustion, unleashed a torrent of arcane energy, her protective amulets pulsing with an ethereal glow, her spells weaving a net of shimmering light that momentarily trapped the vampire, buying Mike precious seconds to gain the upper hand.

The fight raged on, a dizzying blur of movement and impact. Steel clashed against fang, arcane energy against supernatural strength. The rooftop, a precarious battleground high above the city, seemed to tremble under the force of their conflict. The hunters were outnumbered, outmatched, but not outmaneuvered. They fought with the precision of a well-oiled machine, their movements coordinated, their skills complementing one another.

The second encounter took place in the city's underbelly, a network of forgotten tunnels and abandoned subway stations. The darkness here was absolute, broken only by the flickering beams of their flashlights, and the occasional glint of Samson's teeth. Here, the hunters relied on their senses, their instincts, their ancient lore to navigate the treacherous maze, to track their prey. The air hung heavy with the scent of damp earth, decay, and the ever-present metallic tang of blood.

This time, Samson utilized the tunnels' maze-like layout to his advantage, using the shadows and the narrow passages to elude the hunters' grasp. His movements were like whispers in the darkness, his attacks swift and deadly. Mike, utilizing his technological prowess, managed to set up a series of strategically placed sensors and traps, utilizing the city's subterranean network against the vampire. The traps slowed Samson down, giving the hunters a temporary advantage, a brief window of opportunity.

The final showdown occurred on the observation deck of the city's tallest building, a stark, exposed space offering panoramic views of the sprawling city below. The wind howled around them, a chilling reminder of their precarious perch, the city's lights twinkling far below, a million tiny sparks in the vast expanse of the night.

This was it, the culmination of their relentless pursuit, the ultimate clash between hunters and prey, between the forces of light and darkness. Samson, cornered and desperate, unleashed his full fury, his attacks relentless, his movements fueled by a primal, desperate rage. He was faster, stronger, more agile than they had ever witnessed, his fangs dripping with an unnatural venom, his eyes burning with a malevolent intensity.

Mike, Venga, and Ralph, fighting as one, met his assault head-on. Their movements were a whirlwind of coordinated action, their skills honed to perfection. They fought not only with weapons and magic, but also with the strength of their unwavering determination, the loyalty they shared, the memory of their fallen comrade fueling their every action.

The battle raged on, a desperate struggle against overwhelming odds. The hunters fought with a courage born of desperation, their resolve tempered by loss, their will hardened by the intensity of the conflict. They used all their skills, all their resources, all their combined might to take down the fog-vampire, a symbol of the darkness that threatened to engulf their city.

The climax arrived in a blinding flash of light and arcane energy, a chaotic maelstrom of raw power that threatened to rip apart the observation deck. In the end, it was a combination of cunning strategy, superior technology, and a desperate act of self-sacrifice that brought Samson down. Exhausted, wounded, but victorious, the hunters stood amidst the ruins of their battle, the fog-vampire finally vanquished. The city below, unaware of the epic battle fought high above, continued its nightly hum, oblivious to the near-catastrophe that had been averted. The hunters, however, knew that their war was far from over. The shadows lingered, the darkness remained, waiting for its moment to strike again. The night was still young, and the hunt would continue.

The silence that followed Samson's demise was deafening, a stark contrast to the chaotic maelstrom that had preceded it. The observation deck, once a symbol of the city's ambition, now lay in ruins, a testament to the brutal battle that had just transpired. Twisted metal groaned under the weight of the collapsed supports, shards of glass glittered under the pale moonlight, and the lingering scent of ozone hung heavy in the air, a ghostly reminder of the clash of arcane energies.

Mike, leaning against a shattered railing, felt the tremor in his hands, the throbbing ache in his side a dull counterpoint to the adrenaline still coursing through his veins. He gazed down at the city spread out before him, a tapestry of lights twinkling in the vast expanse of the night, each tiny spark representing a life spared from Samson's insatiable hunger. A wave of exhaustion washed over him, threatening to pull him under, but the deep satisfaction of victory held him aloft, a fragile raft in a sea of weariness.

Venga, her face pale but resolute, knelt beside Ralph, who lay unconscious, his chest rising and falling with shallow breaths. The amulet around her neck, usually a vibrant beacon of power, was now dimmed, its glow flickering like a dying ember. The strain of the battle had taken its toll, draining her reserves of arcane energy, leaving her feeling weak and vulnerable. She gently checked Ralph's pulse, a silent prayer escaping her lips. he was alive, but barely.

The weight of their victory settled upon them, heavy and oppressive. They had won, but at what cost? Chet's sacrifice echoed in the desolate landscape of the observation deck, a constant reminder of the fragility of life, the ephemeral nature of triumph. The victory felt hollow, a cruel mockery of their grief, a bitter pill swallowed with a gulp of exhaustion and despair. The cost of their victory was etched into their souls, a permanent scar marking their triumph.

The city lights seemed to dim, their brilliance momentarily eclipsed by the shadow of their loss. The sounds of the city, once a distant hum, now felt amplified, each car horn, each siren, each whispered conversation a stark reminder of the lives that continued, oblivious to the epic battle fought high above. The contrast was jarring, a painful juxtaposition of life and death, of triumph and tragedy. The city, oblivious to their sorrow, continued to breathe, its rhythmic pulse a constant counterpoint to the still, silent figure of their fallen comrade.

As dawn broke, painting the eastern sky with streaks of pale orange and rose, they carefully carried Ralph down from the observation deck, his limp body a heavy burden. The descent was arduous, each step a testament to their exhaustion, their bodies screaming in protest against the strain. They moved through the deserted streets like ghosts, their movements silent, their shadows stretching long and distorted in the pale light of the new day.

The hospital was cold, sterile, a stark contrast to the raw, untamed energy of their rooftop battle. The doctors, their faces grim, worked tirelessly, fighting to save Ralph's life, their efforts a silent tribute to the sacrifices made in the city's defense. Mike and Venga sat by his bedside, their exhaustion evident in their slumped postures, their silence punctuated only by the rhythmic beep of the heart monitor, a fragile heartbeat hanging in the balance.

The days that followed were a blur of medical reports, hushed conversations, and the slow, agonizing process of healing. Ralph eventually recovered, but the experience had left its mark, a shadow of doubt lurking beneath the surface of his brave exterior. The loss of Chet continued to haunt them, a palpable presence in their shared silences, an unsaid word hanging heavy in the air.

Their victory over Samson had brought an end to the immediate threat, but it had also brought to the surface a profound sense of loss, a painful awareness of their mortality. They had faced down a cosmic horror and emerged victorious, but the scars they bore were deep and indelible, a constant reminder of the sacrifices made and the battle still to be fought.

The investigation into Samson's origins and his connection to the city's ley lines continued. The ancient texts, painstakingly deciphered by Chet, revealed a network of supernatural energies coursing beneath the city, a potent force capable of both creation and destruction. Samson was but a pawn in a much larger game, a manifestation of a power they were only beginning to understand.

The hunt for the mastermind behind Samson's actions became their new focus, a relentless pursuit fueled by a mixture of grief, determination, and a growing sense of unease. The city, once safe, now felt vulnerable, the darkness they had momentarily banished looming large in their collective consciousness. They knew that the victory was fragile, temporary, a brief reprieve in a long, ongoing war against the unseen forces that threatened to consume their world. Their victory, hard-won and costly, was just another chapter in an epic saga, a prelude to the battles that lay ahead.

The fog had lifted, but the shadows remained, longer and darker than ever before, and in these shadows, a new threat was taking shape. Their fight against the darkness had not ended; it had merely changed. The city was safe, for now, but the hunters knew that the quiet hum of normalcy held a sinister undercurrent, a deceptive lull before a potentially far greater storm. The next encounter, they knew, might not be as fortunate. The hunters, scarred but resolute, were preparing, awaiting the inevitable return of darkness, their vigil a testament to their commitment, a grim determination etched on their faces. The hunt, it seemed, would never truly end. The city slept, unaware of the watchful eyes that guarded it, the silent guardians ever vigilant, always waiting, always hunting. The war, they knew, had only just begun.

The sterile scent of antiseptic couldn't mask the metallic tang of blood, a phantom smell clinging to Mike's clothes even after multiple showers. He sat by Ralph's bedside, the rhythmic beep of the heart monitor a relentless metronome marking the passage of time. Ralph, pale and gaunt, slept, his breathing shallow, a testament to the brutal fight they'd endured. The bullet wound, though patched, still left a raw, angry crimson line across his chest, a stark reminder of their near-miss. Mike traced the scar on his own arm, a parallel wound mirroring Ralph's, a shared battle-scar, a bond forged in blood and fire. He felt a dull ache in his ribs, a constant throb that reminded him of his own mortality, the fragility of their victory. The victory felt hollow, tainted by the absence of Chet.

Venga sat across from him, her usually vibrant amulet dull, its power drained, mirroring the depletion she felt within herself. The arcane energies she had wielded had left her exhausted, her body weak, her spirit bruised. The strength she had summoned to fight Samson felt like a distant memory, a fading echo of a desperate struggle. She looked at Ralph, her eyes filled with a silent prayer, her face etched with the exhaustion of both physical and magical exertion. The weight of their collective trauma settled heavily in the silence of the hospital room, a palpable presence thicker than the antiseptic air.

Days bled into weeks. Ralph's recovery was slow, arduous. The physical wounds healed, but the psychological scars remained, deep and festering. Nightmares plagued him, vivid replays of the rooftop battle, the chilling scream of Chet, the suffocating weight of Samson's presence. He would wake in a cold sweat, his heart pounding, gasping for air, the echoes of the fight haunting him. Mike and Venga sat with him, offering what comfort they could, sharing their own memories, their own traumas, in a desperate attempt to lighten the burden. Their shared experiences forged a bond stronger than steel, a bond forged in the crucible of shared peril. They understood each other's silent pain, the unspoken language of trauma.

The city, oblivious to their suffering, continued its relentless rhythm. The daily hum of life went on, a stark contrast to the turmoil they had endured. People walked the streets, unaware of the battles fought in the shadows, oblivious to the sacrifices made to protect them. The irony was a sharp sting, a constant reminder of the precarious balance between the mundane and the supernatural. The world had continued, indifferent to their near-death experiences, to their loss.

Mike found himself haunted by Chet's death. Chet, with his quick wit and even quicker reflexes, was more than just a teammate; he was a brother, a friend. Their shared jokes, their inside banter, the easy camaraderie they shared – all reduced to a painful, aching silence. Mike relived their last moments together, the adrenaline-fueled chaos of the fight, the sudden, violent end. The image of Chet, falling from the rooftop, the crimson stain spreading across the concrete, replayed relentlessly in his mind. He felt a crushing guilt, a sense of responsibility for the loss. He'd promised himself, promised Chet, that he'd protect him, and he'd failed.

Venga struggled with the depletion of her magical reserves. The battle with Samson had been a brutal drain on her powers, leaving her feeling weakened, exposed, vulnerable. The amulet around her neck, a source of strength and protection, felt lifeless, a pale imitation of its former vibrant glory. She spent hours meditating, attempting to reconnect with the ancient energies, to replenish her reserves, but the process was slow, agonizing. The weight of their shared trauma, combined with the depletion of her magical abilities, left her feeling emotionally and physically drained.

Ralph's recovery was not merely physical; he found himself grappling with existential questions. He had stared death in the face, had felt the cold grip of mortality, and it had changed him. The near-death experience had shattered his complacency, forcing him to confront his own fears and vulnerabilities. He questioned his faith, his beliefs, the very essence of his existence. The ancient texts they'd deciphered, detailing Samson's connection to the city's ley lines, deepened his fascination with the supernatural, but also instilled a profound sense of awe and respect for the forces they had confronted. His analytical mind, usually so precise and logical, felt overwhelmed by the mysteries of the supernatural world, a universe of potent energies and unseen forces.

The investigation into the mastermind behind Samson's actions consumed their remaining energy. The ancient texts revealed a complex network of supernatural energies, a labyrinthine system of ley lines that pulsed beneath the city. Samson, they realized, was merely a pawn in a larger, more sinister game, a puppet controlled by unseen forces. The hunt for the puppet master was a relentless pursuit, fueled by a mixture of grief, anger, and a burning desire for justice. They knew that the threat hadn't ended with Samson's demise; it had merely shifted, evolved into something more dangerous, more insidious. The city, they realized, was vulnerable, and they were the only ones who could protect it.

The fog had lifted, both literally and metaphorically. But a deeper shadow lingered, a chilling reminder of the darkness that lurked beneath the surface. The city, lulled into a false sense of security, continued to breathe, unaware of the silent guardians watching over it. Mike, Venga, and Ralph, scarred but resolute, prepared for the inevitable return of darkness. They were healers, protectors, hunters. The victory over Samson was a temporary reprieve, a fleeting moment of respite in an ongoing battle against the darkness. Their healing was incomplete, their wounds both physical and emotional, constantly reminding them of the price of their victory, a victory purchased with blood and sacrifice. The war was far from over; the hunt continued. The city slept, unaware of the watchful eyes that guarded it, the silent guardians ever vigilant, always waiting, always hunting. The fight against the unseen forces was an endless cycle, a constant vigilance. The darkness was patient; they would have to be too.

The chipped mug warmed Mike's hands, the lukewarm coffee doing little to soothe the icy chill that still clung to him, a lingering echo of the rooftop battle. He watched the city lights bloom across the valley, a glittering tapestry woven against the inky blackness of the night. It was a beautiful sight, a stark contrast to the brutal reality of their recent ordeal. He thought of Chet, the image still sharp and clear in his mind – the fall, the spreading crimson stain, the silent finality of it all. The guilt, a constant companion, gnawed at him, a persistent ache in his chest that rivaled the dull throb of his own healing ribs.

Venga sat beside him, her gaze fixed on the distant mountains, her usually vibrant amulet now a dull, almost lifeless piece of metal. The effort of drawing on her magical reserves during the fight had left her weakened, not just physically, but spiritually. The ancient energies felt distant, elusive, like a fading whisper on the wind. The silence between them wasn't awkward; it was a shared understanding, a silent acknowledgment of the scars they carried, both visible and unseen.

Ralph, surprisingly, was the most outwardly composed. The physical wounds had healed, but the experience had reshaped him, stripping away layers of complacency and replacing them with a profound understanding of his own mortality. He was different, his usually sharp, analytical mind now tinged with a quiet reverence for the forces they had confronted. The ancient texts they had studied, the intricate connections between the ley lines and Samson's power, had opened up a new world for him, a world of potent energies and ancient mysteries. He was no longer just a tech expert; he was a scholar of the supernatural, his fascination both enthralling and unsettling.

They had dismantled Samson's operation, uncovering a network of hidden lairs and clandestine rituals. The evidence was carefully documented, photographs and recordings carefully catalogued, a testament to the detailed nature of their investigation. They'd found traces of a larger organization, a shadowy cabal pulling the strings, manipulating events from the darkness. Their hunt for the puppet master was far from over, a long, arduous journey into the heart of a hidden world.

Mike traced the faint scar on his arm, a constant reminder of the price of their victory. He'd expected closure, a sense of completion, but instead, he felt a deep sense of unease, a nagging feeling that their work was far from finished. The battle with Samson was just a single engagement in a larger war, a skirmish in a protracted conflict against the forces of darkness.

Venga, ever the pragmatist, focused on rebuilding her strength. She spent hours meditating, drawing on ancient techniques to replenish her depleted energies. The process was slow, painstaking, but she was determined to recover her full potential, to be ready for whatever challenges lay ahead. She studied the texts, poring over the intricate details of the city's ley lines, searching for clues, for weaknesses, for any indication of the enemy's next move.

Ralph, in his own way, was equally focused. He had established a makeshift laboratory in his apartment, a sanctuary of technology and ancient knowledge. He was deciphering more texts, analyzing the data they had collected, seeking patterns, connections, anything that could shed light on the larger organization behind Samson. He was obsessed with understanding the enemy, with unraveling the mysteries that lay at the heart of this hidden conflict. Sleep was a luxury he rarely afforded himself, driven by an insatiable thirst for knowledge, a desperate need to comprehend the forces they had encountered.

Their small team, now a trio bound by shared trauma and unwavering dedication, had become something more than hunters. They were guardians, protectors of the city, a silent shield against the encroaching darkness. They worked in the shadows, their movements unseen, their actions unheard, their only reward the silent gratitude of a city oblivious to the battles fought on its behalf. The risk remained, ever-present, a constant reminder of the fragility of their victory.

One evening, weeks after the final confrontation, they gathered at a small, unassuming diner on the outskirts of Salt Lake City. The aroma of freshly brewed coffee and sizzling bacon was a welcome contrast to the sterile scent of antiseptic that still clung to Mike's memory. They talked, not about the battle, but about the future, about the challenges that lay ahead.

"We need a plan," Venga stated, her voice firm despite the lingering weariness. "Samson was only a pawn. We need to find the ones pulling the strings."

Ralph nodded, his eyes gleaming with an unsettling intensity. "I've been analyzing the data, cross-referencing the texts with the artifacts we recovered. There are patterns emerging, connections I hadn't noticed before. It points to a network far larger than we initially thought, a sophisticated organization with deep roots in this city."

Mike, ever the practical one, focused on the immediate task. "We need resources. We need more people, maybe not hunters, but people who can support us, people who can keep us from being overwhelmed."

The conversation flowed seamlessly, a testament to their evolving understanding. The shared experience had forged a bond stronger than steel, a kinship forged in the crucible of peril. They were more than just a team; they were a family, their loyalty unwavering, their commitment unbreakable.

The city, oblivious to their existence, continued its relentless rhythm. People walked the streets, unaware of the hidden battle raging beneath the surface. The fog had lifted, but a deeper shadow lingered, a chilling reminder of the darkness they were battling. They were the silent sentinels, the unseen guardians, the last line of defense against the forces that threatened to engulf the world in darkness. Their victory over Samson was a momentary reprieve, a fleeting pause in a war that would never truly end. The hunt continued. The shadows deepened. The fight went on, a never-ending struggle between the light and the encroaching darkness, a battle waged in the silent heart of the city. They were the ones who stood between them and oblivion, forever vigilant, forever watchful, forever hunting. The future was uncertain, the challenges immense, but they stood ready, their resolve hardened, their spirits unbroken. They were the hunters, and the hunt would never truly end. The night was long, the darkness profound, but in the hearts of these three warriors, a new beginning flickered – a promise of resilience, of unwavering courage, of an endless pursuit of justice. The city slept, unaware of its silent guardians, ever vigilant, ever watching, ever hunting. The darkness waits; they, too, will wait, ever prepared for the inevitable return of the night.

Years passed. Salt Lake City blossomed, its skyline expanding, its population growing. The vibrant pulse of the city, a relentless rhythm of life, masked the undercurrents of darkness. The fog, once a harbinger of dread, now drifted harmlessly, a wisp of mist clinging to the Wasatch Mountains at dawn. The scars remained, however – not just on the physical landscape, where the remnants of Samson's lair still lay buried beneath the concrete and steel of urban expansion, but also within the hearts of the hunters.

Mike, now a seasoned detective within the Salt Lake City Police Department, often found himself staring at the city lights, a familiar ache in his chest, a reminder of Chet's sacrifice. The routine of his job provided a veneer of normalcy, a shield against the memories that haunted his sleep. He'd built a life, a family, anchoring himself to the mundane, yet the phantom scent of decay, the echo of Samson's guttural whispers, occasionally pierced through the quiet comfort of his domesticity. He carried a worn photograph of Chet in his wallet, a silent tribute to a friendship forged in fire. His new responsibilities included liaising with a small, discreet task force; the city's official recognition of the supernatural, while unofficial and extremely secretive, was a testament to the impact of their work. They focused on smaller threats, the stray manifestations, the lesser evils that still lurked in the shadows, ensuring that the city remained protected. The victories were quieter, the battles less spectacular, but no less crucial.

Venga, her once vibrant amulet gleaming faintly again, became a respected scholar at the University of Utah, her lectures on ancient folklore and occult history subtly weaving in tales of the fight against the shadows. She'd crafted a life devoted to understanding the ancient energies that flowed beneath the city, a life that allowed her to maintain her connection to the supernatural world while nurturing her own sense of peace. Her research, though never officially linked to the hunters' past exploits, provided a valuable understanding of the city's vulnerabilities, silently guiding the city's protectors. The students, fascinated by her tales, never truly understood the depth of her knowledge, or the profound scars it held. She found solace in the classroom, a sanctuary where she could channel her power for good, educating future generations on the enduring struggle against the unseen.

Ralph, ever the restless mind, established a cutting-edge technology company, his expertise in both the physical and metaphysical worlds allowing him to develop advanced surveillance systems and predictive algorithms, silently safeguarding the city against any looming threats. His company, seemingly ordinary in its operations, functioned as a secret arm of the city's defense, subtly deflecting potential dangers before they could manifest. His success allowed him to discreetly fund the hunters' operations, ensuring they had the necessary resources without raising suspicion. The paradox of his life – a successful entrepreneur quietly working to protect the city from the unseen – was a testament to his resilience and his unwavering commitment to their shared purpose. He often joked about trading in his soldering iron for a stake, a testament to the lighter side of their shared trauma, yet the underlying seriousness remained.

The city's unseen guardians worked in the shadows, a silent network protecting Salt Lake City from the lurking darkness. The city's mayor, discreetly informed by Mike's department, allocated small, unassuming budgets to initiatives that would support the team without ever explicitly acknowledging the nature of their work. This delicate balance – maintaining the illusion of normalcy while quietly ensuring the city's safety – became the new normal. The unspoken understanding between the city's leaders and its protectors represented a fragile, yet powerful, alliance. The threat of another Samson remained, a dark possibility lingering at the edge of their awareness.

Their methods evolved. They relied less on brute force and more on subtle interventions, on anticipating threats before they could materialize. They learned to identify patterns, to read the subtle shifts in the city's energy, to sense the presence of the supernatural long before it manifested in visible ways. Their knowledge of the city's ley lines became a crucial asset, a network of energy they could both harness and protect. They became the city's silent guardians, weaving a tapestry of protection that was invisible to most but felt by those who were attuned to the unseen.

The annual Salt Lake City Arts Festival became an important occasion. Each year, a specific artwork, seemingly innocuous to the casual observer, held a hidden significance for the hunters. They'd embed subtle energy signatures within the pieces, acting as wards or trackers, allowing them to monitor the city's ley lines and detect any unusual energy fluctuations. This intricate system, woven into the fabric of the city's cultural life, was a testament to their creativity and foresight.

Fifteen years later, Mike stood on the same rooftop where they'd faced Samson. The city spread before him, a breathtaking panorama of lights against the darkening sky. His hair was graying, the lines on his face deeper, but his eyes still held the same sharp intensity. He wasn't hunting vampires anymore; he was mentoring a new generation of guardians, a small team of young individuals who were beginning to understand the depth of the city's secrets. He'd selected them carefully, seeking those with an innate sensitivity to the unseen, those with the resilience to face the darkness and the courage to protect their city.

Venga, now in her seventies, held a small, intimate gathering in her garden every year. It was an occasion where she'd share stories of the past, her words tinged with a melancholic wisdom that both captivated and unsettled her listeners. The garden, overflowing with flowers representing various protective properties according to ancient lore, became a symbol of resilience and renewal. The tales served not just as a reminder of the past, but as a warning and a preparation for the future. The gathering, shrouded in secrecy, served as a powerful reminder of the continued need for vigilance.

Ralph, with his company a global powerhouse in technological innovation, continued his quiet support. His donations, often disguised as philanthropic contributions, funded research into the supernatural and ensured that the city remained prepared for any unforeseen challenges. He'd designed a new system of energy sensors, subtly integrated into the city's infrastructure, silently monitoring for any disturbance in the ley lines. This cutting-edge technology, a silent guardian of the city, stood as a testament to his unwavering dedication.

The city's future, though uncertain, held a glimmer of hope. The hunters were gone, but their legacy lived on, a silent echo in the heart of Salt Lake City. The darkness still lurked, its presence a constant, yet muted, threat. The city slept, unaware of the silent guardians who watched over it, ready to face the shadows whenever they emerged from the abyss. The vigil continued, a timeless battle between light and darkness, a never-ending struggle fought in the heart of a city that remained blissfully ignorant of its own salvation. The city was safe, for now, protected by the legacy of the hunters, by the quiet vigilance of those who carried the torch forward. The hunt, in its quiet, unseen form, continued.

Glossary

Ley Line: A mythical line of energy running through the earth, often associated with supernatural activity.

Fog Vampire (Samson): A rare species of vampire that manifests within dense fog, feeding on life force rather than blood. Its power is intrinsically linked to the ley lines.

Amulet of Venga: An ancient artifact, imbued with protective energies, capable of sensing and warding off supernatural entities.

Metaphysical Technology: Technology designed to interact with and manipulate supernatural energies.

About the Author

Willie S. is an aspiring author who immerses himself in sci-fi, fantasy, and speculative fiction, crafting tales that transport readers to uncharted realms of imagination. His writing serves as both a creative outlet and a bridge to share the intricacies of his envisioned worlds with others. With a passion for exploring the metaphysical and delving into the unknown, Willie infuses his work with themes that challenge boundaries and inspire wonder. Every story he pens is a testament to his belief in the power of storytelling to connect hearts and minds, shedding light on the extraordinary hidden within the ordinary. Through his art, he hopes to ease his spirit and awaken the dreamer in all of us.

Samson Bordeau is on the hunt. He is also hunted, and he knows it. An expert team that is always learning and refocusing their strengths and weaknesses is out to find out what is going on in Salt Lake. With the help of each other, and their knowledge, this may be their most challenging chase yet.